ALSO BY M A

Blind Justice (Novella)

Cruel Justice (Book #1)

Mortal Justice (Novella)

Impeding Justice (Book #2)

Final Justice (Book #3)

Foul Justice (Book #4)

Guaranteed Justice (Book #5)

Ultimate Justice (Book #6)

Virtual Justice (Book #7)

Hostile Justice (Book #8)

Tortured Justice (Book #9)

Rough Justice (Book #10)

Dubious Justice (Book #11)

Calculated Justice (Book #12)

Twisted Justice (Book #13)

Justice at Christmas (Short Story)

Justice at Christmas 2 (novella)

Prime Justice (Book #14)

Heroic Justice (Book #15)

Shameful Justice (Book #16)

Immoral Justice (Book #17)

Toxic Justice (Book #18)

Overdue Justice (Book #19)

Unfair Justice (a 10,000 word short story)

Irrational Justice (a 10,000 word short story)

Seeking Justice (a 15,000 word novella)

Caring For Justice (a 24,000 word novella)

Savage Justice (a 17,000 word novella Featuring THE UNICORN)

Vile Justice (A 17,000 word novella)

Gone in Seconds (Justice Again series Book #1)

Ultimate Dilemma (Justice Again series Book #2)

Clever Deception (co-written by Linda S Prather)

Tragic Deception (co-written by Linda S Prather)

Sinful Deception (co-written by Linda S Prather)

Forever Watching You (DI Miranda Carr thriller)

Wrong Place (DI Sally Parker thriller #1)

No Hiding Place (DI Sally Parker thriller #2)

Cold Case (DI Sally Parker thriller#3)

Deadly Encounter (DI Sally Parker thriller #4)

Lost Innocence (DI Sally Parker thriller #5)

Goodbye, My Precious Child (DI Sally Parker #6)

Web of Deceit (DI Sally Parker Novella with Tara Lyons)

The Missing Children (DI Kayli Bright #1)

Killer On The Run (DI Kayli Bright #2)

Hidden Agenda (DI Kayli Bright #3)

Murderous Betrayal (Kayli Bright #4)

Dying Breath (Kayli Bright #5)

Taken (Kayli Bright #6 coming March 2020)

The Hostage Takers (DI Kayli Bright Novella)

No Right to Kill (DI Sara Ramsey #1)

Killer Blow (DI Sara Ramsey #2)

The Dead Can't Speak (DI Sara Ramsey #3)

Cozy Mystery Series

Murder at the Wedding

Murder at the Hotel

Murder by the Sea

Tempting Christa (A billionaire romantic suspense co-authored by Tracie Delaney #1)

Avenging Christa (A billionaire romantic suspense co-authored by Tracie Delaney #2)

ACKNOWLEDGMENTS

Thank you as always to my rock, Jean, I'd be lost without
you in my life.

Special thanks as always go to @studioenp for their superb cover
design expertise.

My heartfelt thanks go to my wonderful editor Emmy Ellis, my
proofreaders Joseph, Barbara and Jacqueline for spotting all the
lingering nits.

To Mary, gone, but never forgotten. I hope you found the peace you
were searching for, my dear friend.

PROLOGUE

*L*ife was a breeze and didn't get any better than this. Ray Thatcham lay on the deck of the boat with his arm around a busty brunette who'd been working alongside him for a little while. "Get me another cocktail, will you, doll?"

"Wow, I've never seen someone drink so many. Want the same?"

"I think I'll have the Hawaiian Dream now. The ingredients are on the list inside the drinks' cabinet."

"I hate having to create ones I don't know, can't you stick with the Manhattans?"

He clutched a handful of her hair and viciously pulled her towards him. "Lady, any backchat and you're gonna piss me off, got that?"

Tina cried out in pain and placed a hand on his chest to push away from him. Tears welled up. "I'm sorry, baby. There's no need to get angry with me."

He smiled, covering the anger still bubbling beneath the surface. "Don't test my patience. Life's stressful enough as it is right now, without you adding to it. Now get me my drink and then come back here and make it up to me." He let go of her hair.

She leaned forward and gave him a lingering kiss. "Something to keep you satisfied until I get back, baby."

"I can't wait. Now get out of here." He smacked her on the arse. The boat was moored up; he was intent on topping up his tan today and just chilling.

She giggled her way across the deck and into the cabin below. He closed his eyes, once again thinking how lucky he was to be alive. He'd achieved a hell of a lot throughout his thirty-two years on this earth which had amounted to this year being the one that had brought him double the profits and expanded his business portfolio to another level.

He let out a contented sigh. The sun blazing down on his already tanned skin only enriched the day further.

Tina padded towards him again. He snuck a quick look through a half-opened eye. *If she kept her mouth shut and her legs open all the time, I wouldn't mind having her around full-time. Maybe that's down to me to train her properly.*

She placed the cocktail on the deck beside him and kissed his cheek.

He groaned his appreciation as her hands slid down his body to his trunks. "Oh yeah, baby, that's it." His eyes squeezed tight, his anticipation growing along with his erection.

Tina let out a squeal, and something cold ran the length of his chest instead of her hand. His eyes shot open to find two bruisers standing on the deck. One of them had his arm around her throat, the other stood two feet away, holding a gun.

He sat up. "Hey, what the fuck is going on here?" Unfortunately, he recognised the men and had an inkling this wasn't going to end well.

"The boss sent us down here to check on you. Have you made the delivery yet?" the bulkier goon who was aiming the gun at his chest asked.

He swallowed the saliva filling his mouth. "Yeah, well, not exactly. I was going to do it this afternoon."

The goon sneered and shot the girl in the leg then turned the gun on him again.

Tina screamed. Her legs gave way beneath her, but the goon throttling her never moved an inch. She soon returned to her position as the tears slipped down her flushed cheeks.

"Ray, help me!" she whimpered.

In truth, he couldn't give a flying fuck what happened to her, his survival uppermost in his mind, not hers.

"See, the boss is going to be pissed with you for delaying his instructions. The drugs were supposed to be delivered by twelve at the latest. Instead, here you are, thirty minutes past the deadline, sunning yourself with a scrawny, brainless bitch stroking your knob."

"Hey, give me a break, it's been a tough week. I'm entitled to some downtime, man."

The guy lashed out, pistol-whipping him. The sound of breaking bone filled the air. "Not the fucking attitude the boss expects from you. Where's the stuff?"

He held his aching jaw, determined not to let the guy know how much pain was coursing through his body. "What? I said I'd deliver it and I will. I'll get ready now and do it."

"You've had your chance and you've royally screwed up. The thing is, the boss doesn't trust you. He sent us to follow you, and I've already reported back to him, informed him you've let him down. He's given us instructions to pick up the stuff and, well…to deal with you and the slag."

"No. I'm sorry. Look, guys, what'll it take for you to turn a blind eye? I've got money. Go on, let us go, tell your boss the stuff has been delivered and I'll deposit a hundred grand in each of your accounts."

The two men glanced at each other.

The one holding Tina raised an eyebrow. "Sounds good to me, mate."

"All right, just this once. You can make the transfer now, right?"

"Yeah, I'll get my phone, it's in the cabin."

"I'll get it, tell me where it is."

"In the bedroom, on the bedside cabinet," Ray replied, relieved that he'd somehow managed to persuade the men to accept the payoff. Money, the root of all evil and the motivator of many.

The goon disappeared inside and emerged a few seconds later. In his absence, Ray didn't move, not an ounce of compassion or inclination to try to attempt to rescue Tina. Her life meant nothing compared to his. He was all about sole survival, it had been that way since childhood, since his parents had dumped him outside the church when he was just a nipper, barely out of nappies.

He'd grown up living in various foster homes, not one of them caring enough to want to adopt him, which suited him fine. He drifted between families, causing problems if he didn't gel with the adults, which always resulted in him moving on to the next one. No one in the system gave the kids credit for having a say in their own destiny. He'd made his own way in life since, made millions in the process by grafting hard and living life to the full when he had a spare few minutes. He'd accomplished his millionaire status at the tender age of twenty-one. How many people could have that tattoo emblazoned on their calf, like he had? Not many he had crossed paths with, that was for sure.

The two goons gave him their bank details and high-fived each other over the transactions when they went through.

Two hundred grand is a drop in the ocean, I can make that money back within a month.

"Right, gents, if you wouldn't mind leaving us now, Tina and I were about to have a good time, if you know what I mean."

The one holding Tina around the throat let his hand drop to her heaving, well-proportioned breasts and fondled each one roughly through the flimsy material.

She squirmed and whined, "Please, let me go. You've had your money."

The man holding the gun shook his head. "You need to learn to keep your mouth shut, slapper." He aimed the gun at Ray.

"No, wait. That wasn't in the agreement. Kill her if you need to, but let me go, guys, there's more money where that came from."

The gun went off anyway. Ray took a bullet to his side. His mouth dropped open. The plea running through his head failed to form into actual words. *Shit! What do I do now?* He was used to getting his own way once he'd paraded his wealth to coerce someone. None of that seemed to matter with these guys. He clutched his hand to the wound and gasped. Blood trickled through his fingers, and the agony intensified, although he was too much in shock for the pain to register at first. It didn't take him long to realise that if he didn't get medical help soon, he was going to die. "Jesus, man, why did you do that? I need to get to the hospital and quickly."

"What you need and what you're gonna get are two different things, pal," the bulkier man said, his gaze drifting to the Thames behind them. "Shit, we've got company."

The other goon swept the girl into his arms and took her below deck. He returned carrying a dark-blue towelling robe which he flung at Ray. "Put it on."

Ray slipped it over one shoulder and struggled to put his arm through the other. The police boat got closer. *How do I play this? Dob them in to the coppers, my arch enemies over the years, or what?*

"You there, on the *River Princess*, prepare for us to come aboard." The voice was insistent even through the megaphone.

"Let them on and we'll deal with them," the man with the gun said.

"What does that mean?" Ray asked, his voice high-pitched, the strain evident.

The man grinned, tucked his gun in the waistband of his trousers and fastened his jacket to hide the bulge.

The police boat moored behind them, and two young officers boarded the boat and joined them on the deck. "We've received a call about gunshots coming from this boat. Care to tell us what's going on?"

"Sorry? I don't know what you're talking about. My associates and I were in the process of having a meeting."

The young officer's brow rose, and he pointed at the deck. "You'll be telling me next that's tomato ketchup."

"Oh that, no, I cut my foot when I went for a dip in the river earlier."

The officer chewed his lip and shook his head. "Don't give me that bullshit. Open your robe."

"I will not," Ray replied indignantly.

The officer took a step towards him and yanked the robe open and grabbed his Taser at the same time, but it was too late. The goon with the gun whipped out his weapon and fired off two shots, each of them hitting their targets. Both officers dropped to the deck. One of them, the one who had the courage to approach Ray, writhed in pain at his feet.

The officer reached out a hand and begged, "Stop, don't do this."

The gunman silenced him with another two shots to the chest.

"Shit, shit, shit…what the fuck did you go and do that for?" Ray paced the deck.

"Don't fuckin' question my ethics, shitface. We need to get out of here. Start up the boat."

"No way. I need to get to the hospital. I'm losing too much blood to steer this thing."

"You'll do as I say or I'll finish you off here and now, it's your choice."

Ray shook his head and sighed. From what he could tell, he had no other option available to him.

He took up his position in the cockpit and started up the engine. The goons moved the coppers' bodies to the rear and untied the police vessel, setting it adrift. They headed down the narrow part of the river. Ray's eyes were everywhere, watching the pedestrians strolling along the riverbank with not a care in the world, while he was bricking it and losing blood fast by the look of things.

Jesus, why did I have to let my greed take over? I knew I was out of my depth getting involved in the drug side of things. Shit! They're not going to let me get away with this, they'll kill me next. Fuck!

"Where are we heading?" the guy with the gun asked.

"I thought it would be better to get away from there ASAP. We don't want more cops showing up, do we?"

"Good point. But where are we going now?"

"Heading downriver. I can moor up again soon, if that's what you want. Hey, man, I'm bleeding out here, I really need to go to hospital with the girl."

"Dream on, mate, it ain't gonna happen."

Ray decided to push harder on the throttle. The boat surged forward, and the gunman lost his footing. He slammed into the door, and the gun skittered across the floor to Ray's feet. He bent to pick it up. The guy twigged what was happening and pounced on Ray. The gun went off in the ensuing fight between the two men. It didn't take long for the other goon to appear, and between them, the two men overpowered Ray.

They took it in turns to slam their fists into his gut and his face. He doubled over in pain. Sirens wailed behind; yet another police boat was on their tail.

"Fucking stop messing about. If we don't outrun them then we'll all be going down for murder, you hear me?" the gunman shouted in Ray's face, baring his teeth as his lip curled up into a ferocious snarl.

Ray swallowed hard. "But I had nothing to do with it."

The guy hit his temple with the gun. Ray's gaze blurred. The boat bumped into a smaller craft coming in the opposite direction.

"What the fuck are you doing?" The gunman prodded the gun into Ray's side, into his wound.

"Ouch! Shit, it's not my fault, my vision is blurred."

The gunman threw his weapon to the other goon. "Watch him. If he moves, fucking kill the bastard. I'm going to have to steer this thing, it's our only chance of getting out of here."

"Do you know what you're doing?" Ray asked, fearing not only for his own safety but that of his new three-quarter-mill acquisition.

"Fuck off! How difficult can it be?"

"It's harder than you think." Ray peered over his shoulder. "They're gaining on us."

"Here, you take her then. No funny business or the girl gets it."

"I swear. We need to go faster. Brace yourselves."

The boat lunged forward at last. Their speed was greater than that of the police cruiser behind them.

The river widened, much to Ray's relief. "We've got this. They're losing speed rapidly, cowards." He laughed.

"Just get us to shore in one piece. Round the next bend, pull over when you can and we'll leg it."

7

"Shit! We've got no chance of escaping. We're doomed," Ray shouted above the whine of the engine.

"We're sunk with that attitude. Do your best. Be prepared to jump, Stitch."

Stitch stared at him. "Are you fucking crazy? I ain't jumping off no speeding boat."

The other man grasped Stitch's throat and pulled him close, their noses almost touching. "All right, fucking go to jail then, see if I care. You keep my name out of this, though, or I'll hunt you down. I have a number of mates doing time."

"All right, mate. Less of the frigging threats."

"I hate to interrupt," Ray said, "but the bend is almost upon us."

As soon as the boat disappeared around the curve in the river, one of the goons produced a knife. He didn't hesitate and slashed Ray across the throat. Then the two men raced onto the deck. The girl appeared from below and screamed.

The boat was out of control. Ray had slumped over the controls and pushed the throttle to its max.

In his dazed state, he could just make out the two goons standing on the bow getting ready to jump. He didn't know what happened next.

The loss of blood sent him into unconsciousness…

1

_K_aty stretched and ran a hand over AJ's taut muscles. "I wish I had abs like yours." She snuggled into him.

He kissed her on the temple and hugged her tightly. "How many times do I have to tell you? There's nothing wrong with your bloody figure. And look what it has produced, a beautiful daughter."

Katy let out a small sigh. "She is perfect, isn't she?"

"Just like her mum." He used all his strength to pull her on top of him.

Katy stared down at the man she'd lost her heart to over six years before, virtually the day she'd joined the Met police after transferring from the Manchester force.

They had got engaged and had Georgina within a year of meeting, and now, after a discreet service at the weekend, they were an official couple in the eyes of God, husband and wife for their sins. They were regretting not telling their respective parents. Not so much hers, but his mother and father were bound to chuck their dummies out of the pram. His father was a Member of Parliament and had a reputation to uphold. But AJ had made sure he wasn't reliant on his family's wealth a long time ago, hence him joining the police force at a young age. He'd given all that up to become a house-husband and care for their delightful daughter, knowing that Katy, now an inspector again, would be bringing in more of a salary than he could earn.

"You always were a charmer. I suppose we'd better ring our parents at the weekend. Can't say I'm looking forward to doing that."

"Let's get used to the idea first, just you, me and Georgina. I love you, Mrs Jackson."

"About that, do you think I should change my name at work?"

"Why not? It's up to you, no pressure from me."

"I'm in two minds about it. Maybe sticking with my single name will keep you guys safe."

"I don't understand."

"Criminals are getting worse, you know that. Every day, the length and breadth of the country, we hear an officer has been either abducted or hurt because they were connected with a certain case. I'd hate for anything to happen to you or Georgina because a criminal did their research into my family."

"True enough. Although, if they were that determined to trace us, they'd find a way, no matter what name you go under."

"Thanks for putting my mind at ease about that." She laughed and swiped his chest. "I'd better jump in the shower."

"Yeah, which means I have to get up and sort our little munchkin out ready for playschool."

Katy bent to kiss him. "You're the best husband and father around."

"I know." He grinned.

"You're also very vain, but I love you all the same."

*K*aty left their three-bedroom semi-detached house, which AJ managed to maintain beautifully, around thirty minutes later and drove to the police station which she affectionally called 'her other home'. To Katy, the station really felt like the home where she spent more time than her proper home.

She waved at Charlie who was just getting out of her Ford Fiesta. "Hi, how's it going today, Charlie?"

"Hey, I'm fine. Enough about me, did you do it?"

Katy held up her ring finger. "Yep. Sorry we couldn't invite you. I hope you understand it was a quiet affair? Just me, AJ and Georgina. We grabbed two witnesses off the street." She cringed, admitting that fact.

"Wow, you did? I'm fine about it. I know someone who'll be disappointed when I tell her, though."

Katy cringed. "Your mum, right?"

"Yep, she and Tony will be devastated they weren't there to share your happy day."

"I'll give her a call this morning, in between going through the post. It'll give me a break from the mundane. Do you really think she's going to be angry with me?"

"Nah, she'll be fine. A tad upset, but on the whole, she'll be overjoyed for you."

"Come on, you can buy your new boss a cup of coffee to celebrate her nuptials."

They entered the building.

The desk sergeant, Mick Crawford, acknowledged them with a nod. "Morning, ladies. What a fine day it is."

"You're full of sunshine today, Mick, any reason for that?"

"Not really. I thought it would make a change to come to work in a positive frame of mind this morning."

"Always good to break your routine now and again," Katy responded, grinning.

"Cheeky. Have a good day."

There was a twinkle in his eye that sent a chill running up Katy's spine. In the past, if anyone dared to utter those particular words, her day usually turned out to be the complete opposite.

They walked up the stairs, nattering as they went. At the top they found DCI Roberts waiting for them. "Morning, ladies. Did you have a good weekend?"

"Yes, thanks, boss," Charlie replied shyly.

"I did, thanks. I have some news. AJ and I tied the knot."

Sean Roberts' mouth gaped open for a second or two. "No way! Should I be offended that you didn't invite me?"

"No one came, not even our parents. Actually, they still don't know. We're intending to break the news this weekend, if nothing drastic happens in the meantime."

"Bloody hell, have you guys got a death wish? I can't see AJ's folks being happy when you tell them."

Katy hitched up her right shoulder. "What's done is done. They'll have to suck it up, won't they? It's our life, as the saying goes, we're old enough to know better."

"Yeah, but it should've probably been a grand affair in their eyes, Katy."

"Which was why we decided to keep it quiet. We thought long and hard and figured ultimately the day should be about the three of us, and it was perfect, just perfect."

"Do we get to see any photos?"

"Soon, I promise."

"Okay, now you've dealt me that shock first thing in the morning, I suppose we'd all better start our day. How are you settling in, Charlie?"

"Really well, I think." Charlie faced Katy for reassurance.

"Best partner I've had, apart from her mother, that is," Katy assured him with a satisfied smile.

"Good to hear. You have huge shoes to fill, make sure that fact doesn't overwhelm you, Charlie. If you need any guidance, don't be afraid to ask Katy, or me, come to that. My door will always be open for you, should you need it."

Charlie's cheeks coloured up. "Thank you, sir."

Katy smiled, and the three of them separated.

"He's mellowed over the years, hasn't he?" Charlie murmured.

Katy pushed through the door to the incident room, disappointed to see they were the first to arrive. "He has. Your mum told me he used to be a right bastard to her when he first showed up. You know they had a fling years ago, don't you?"

"Yeah, Mum told me she passed Sean up to be with Dad, and look how that turned out."

"How is your dad?"

"Still wandering through life in a confused state. He picks up a job here and there and the odd woman along the way, too."

"You don't sound too impressed by his behaviour."

"I'm not. I keep out of his way most of the time. I love him, of course I do. I don't think I like him too much, though. Does that sound harsh?"

"Not in my eyes. By all accounts, he didn't treat Lorne very well when they were married."

"You don't have to tell me that. They thought they hid the arguments and the snide comments from me. Nothing could be further from the truth. I suppose that's why I rebelled as a teenager."

"Shit! You should've told Lorne, she would have probably left your dad sooner rather than put you through all that turmoil."

"She did her best for me, they both did, in their own way."

Katy decided that Charlie seemed uncomfortable discussing her mother and father's relationship so called a halt to the conversation. "I'll be in the office. White with one sugar, when you get around to buying the coffees." She smiled and pushed open the door and let out an agonised groan. Her desk was overflowing with damn paperwork. Most of it belonged to her predecessor who had thrown in the towel and left it for Katy the day she'd retired.

She opened the office window, the heat hitting her with force. She sat behind her desk and sifted through the post first. Charlie came in a few minutes later.

"Here you go. I've even brought you a digestive biscuit. Now, you can take that as sucking up to the new boss or you could see it as a friend sharing their lot with you. Either way, you're welcome."

"Thanks, as much as I appreciate the gesture, please don't make a habit of it. I still have a few pounds of baby fat to shift, and yes, Georgina is five now."

"Oops, hey, you look fine to me. Don't be so hard on yourself."

"Thanks. Now I know what a good liar you are, just like your mum. Talking of which, I'm going to ring her now."

"I'll leave you to it. Send her my love, tell her I'll ring her in the next couple of days." Charlie smiled and left the room.

Katy sipped her coffee. It was just to her liking—her new partner was going to stand the test of time, after all. She nibbled on the tempting biscuit and picked up the desk phone to dial the number which she took from her mobile contacts.

"Hello."

"Why hello, would it be possible to speak to the lady of the house about a new cosmetic range we've developed from dog poo?" Katy couldn't hold back the laughter any longer.

"Katy Foster, is that you?"

"No, it's not. Guess again."

"What? You definitely sound like her. Who is this?"

"This is Mrs Katy Jackson, ha, fooled you."

"Bloody nutter. You had me going there. Wait…you haven't?"

"I ruddy well have."

"Oh, Katy, I'm so thrilled for you. Hang on…Tony, come here, you'll never guess what…Katy and AJ have got married. Isn't it exciting?"

"It's the best news ever, Katy, congratulations, love," Tony shouted from somewhere off in the distance.

"Thanks, guys. I was a little doubtful about ringing you, thought you'd tear me off a strip for not inviting you to the wedding."

"Well, now that you mention it, I am a bit miffed. Have we upset you?"

"Oh, Lorne, it's nothing like that. Even our parents didn't attend. We haven't told them yet. We're doing that at the weekend."

"Oh my God, you're taking a major risk there."

"I know. Enough about me, how's life down on the farm?" Katy chuckled.

"It's hardly a farm. We're in the process of building more kennels, and I know we said we wouldn't create a rescue centre again, but I think that's the route we're taking. How's the new recruit settling in?"

"How cool. I knew you would. She's doing fabulously well. I've put her forward for her sergeant's exam. Not sure if she's told you that or not, oops! Maybe I shouldn't have mentioned it."

"Don't be silly. Of course she's told me, we were both thrilled to hear it. Fingers crossed for her. It'll make a difference to her financially. They could do with the money as Brandon doesn't earn that much being a plumber."

"I thought they did well?"

"Depends who you work for, I suppose. He works in the family business, and I think it's struggling. But I haven't told you that."

"My lips are sealed, you can count on me. Does Tony love it there?"

"Yep. He keeps having a go at me, insisting we should've moved to Norfolk years ago. Now we're living next door to Sally, it's just perfect."

"What's the betting you get roped in to doing some police work up there?"

"Funny you should say that…Sally has asked me and Tony if we fancy delving into a case she's just solved. The perp has killed numerous victims over the years, and apparently there are likely dozens more the police don't know about. She wants us to try and find out who the vics are."

"Really? Sounds intriguing and daunting at the same time. Will you do it?"

"We're still debating it. It's probably on the cards, though. Carol rang the other day, told me to pass on her best wishes to you and also wanted to mention that she's available if you should need her and her psychic abilities going forward."

"Umm…well, you know how I feel about that side of things. Let me ponder that for a while. I know Charlie is close to her, I can see her possibly twisting my arm to use her in the future."

"She's a good egg, don't discount using her out of hand."

"I won't. I'm not as against the idea as I used to be. We'll see what happens. Right, I'd better crack on with this damn paperwork, you know what it's like first thing in the morning around here."

"Hey, I bet it's preferable to mucking out the kennels on a daily basis."

"I doubt it. At least you get to play ball with the inmates afterwards."

They both laughed.

"True enough. I'm always on the end of the phone if you need my help with anything, you know that, don't you?"

"I do. Now bugger off. Have a good day."

"I can take a hint. Speak soon, and send my congratulations to AJ and Georgina, too. Don't forget you have an open invitation to visit us."

"I appreciate that more than you know, Lorne. It was lovely catching up. Much love." Katy ended the call, and the phone rang immediately. "DI Katy Foster," she replied without hesitation.

"It's Mick on reception, ma'am. There's been a major incident that I think you would be interested in."

"I would, would I? Which is?"

"Sometime yesterday afternoon, there was a crash on the Thames."

"Okay, what does that have to do with the Murder Squad, Mick?"

"All right. I'm hearing things on the grapevine that I think you should be hearing."

"You're not making any sense. Run that by me again, if you would?"

Mick ran through what they knew about the incident and sighed. "Now do you see?"

"Okay. Charlie and I will go over there now. I take it the pathologist and SOCO will be finished by now, right?"

"I think SOCO are still at the scene."

"Thanks for the info."

Katy left the office and surveyed the incident room, pleased to see the rest of the team had arrived and had got to work.

"Listen up, folks. News just in that an incident occurred on the Thames yesterday afternoon. Charlie and I are going to take a trip out there to see what actually went on. Karen, can you see what you can discover on the system? Ring me as soon as you find anything."

"I'll get on it now."

Katy and Charlie left the building and drove to the crime scene.

"Mum sends you her love," Katy announced during the drive.

"Is she okay? Last I heard she was debating whether to help DI Parker with a cold case up there."

"Yeah, she told me. She'll do it, I have no doubts about that. If she's considering it, she'll find it hard not to get involved."

"Yep, I think the same."

"She's so damn proud of you, Charlie."

"Aww…that's wonderful to hear. I've done my best to remain level-headed over the years. I think it has paid off in my personal and professional life so far."

"Things can only get better for you. Having a supportive partner is an added bonus, too, take my word for that."

"AJ is to be admired, giving up a career to raise a child. Not every man is up to the task. Dad did his best but failed once I hit my teens."

"His heart was probably in the right place. Your mum used to tell me how difficult it was for him to get back to having a career. He was a mechanic, wasn't he?"

"Still is, off and on. When the work dries up, he'll do anything that's on offer. Enough about personal stuff, I've had my fill for the day. It's being in work mode that gets my heart pumping."

"I hear you. We're almost there, judging by the black smoke ahead of us."

"And this happened yesterday?"

"Yep, hard to believe it's still burning."

The scene was cordoned off. Two uniformed officers guarded the perimeter against the burgeoning crowd, all straining their necks for a closer look.

"Why can't people get on with their miserable lives?" Katy complained. She pressed the key fob to lock the car and strode towards the barrier.

After flashing their warrant cards, Katy and Charlie dipped under the tape and made their way over to the SOCO technicians working the scene.

James Baldwin, the head SOCO on site, smiled at them. "Hi, I wondered when one of your team would show up."

Katy shrugged. "It would have been a lot sooner if someone had bothered to call us. Can you give me a quick rundown on what we have here? There seems to be some confusion as to whether it was an accident or something else."

"I'm not surprised. As you can see, it's still burning, keeps erupting every time the fire brigade leaves the scene, yet to be determined why that is. In between time, members of my team have managed to climb aboard. That's when things escalated more into your realms."

"How so?"

"We found four bodies on board. Three males and one female."

"Okay, what aren't you telling me?"

"It would appear that the three males were murdered."

Katy faced the boat. "Are you telling me the female committed the murders then got trapped on the boat?"

"Possibly. We're still trying to ascertain what went on. There are no witnesses from what we can tell, which is going to make life awkward for us."

"What about IDs? Anything?"

"Two of the males are river police officers."

"Really? What the hell were they doing on board?"

He shrugged. "Yet to be determined. You might want to check with your associates on that one."

"We will, don't worry. What type of injuries are we talking about? Fire related or something more sinister?"

"The two officers received gunshot wounds to the heart. Instantaneous death likely but yet to be confirmed. The other man had his throat cut."

"Crikey, any weapons found?"

"Nothing as yet. The boat hit the bank pretty hard, therefore, we've got a dive team coming out to search the river surrounding the vessel."

"What about the woman?"

"She had a gunshot wound to the right leg and a massive head injury. The pathologist seemed to think she walloped her head on the metal railing at the front of the boat. There are blood stains to corroborate her assumption."

Katy glanced around the area. There was a footpath running on either side of the river. "Hmm…okay, I can't believe there were no witnesses. Look at the number of people standing around here, rubbernecking the scene. I'm sure these footpaths are used regularly by pedestrians, dog walkers, people using a shortcut to work possibly. Charlie, we need to contact uniform, get them to canvass the area, knocking on doors." She pointed at the few of the houses dotted around the area, a few hundred feet away. "Someone must have seen or heard something. Bloody hell, gunshots were fired, for God's sake!" Katy tutted and breathed deeply to quell her rising frustrations.

"I'll get that organised." Charlie left the area to speak to the uniformed officers standing at the cordon. One of them got on the radio. Charlie nodded and returned. "All done. Backup should be here soon."

"Good. James, all right if we go aboard the boat?"

He adamantly shook his head. "No way, sorry, it's far too dangerous."

"Because it keeps bursting into flames?"

"Yep. I've made arrangements for the woman to be lifted out of the water. I'm hoping that'll happen this afternoon. We'll take her back and give her a thorough examination when we return to base."

"I understand. I'm not happy about it but I completely understand the logic behind it."

"Bear with us. Maybe you could pay us a visit tomorrow, have a mooch around then? The thing is, we don't know how much diesel is left in the fuel tank. Once we drain it, the vessel will be a lot safer for us to examine."

"Yep, I agree. Anything else for us? Do we know to whom the boat is registered?"

"Yes, I did manage to uncover that nugget of information for you. Ray Thatcham, I Googled him. Apparently, he's a local businessman. Lots on the internet about his wealth, the fast cars he drives et cetera."

"Does he match one of the victims?"

"As far as I can tell, yes. You might want to hold off on breaking the news to the family until the post-mortem has been performed. Patti Fletcher is in the process of doing that now, I believe."

"That's great news. She shouldn't take long. I'll leave it a while before I chase her up, wouldn't want to contact her midway through."

"Very wise. She wasn't in the best of moods when she attended the scene yesterday afternoon."

"Any idea why?"

"Nope. Maybe it was her time of the month."

Katy shook her head. "Did those words really tumble out of your mouth, James? Shame on you. I've never taken you for a sexist pig in the past."

"Ouch! What did I say?" He seemed genuinely offended by Katy's harsh words.

"How come when women have an off day, men generally put their foul mood down to their menstrual cycle, and yet when guys are having a bad day, those around them have to shrug it off as just one of those days?"

He held up his gloved hands and admitted, "Sorry, I stand corrected. My bad."

Katy swiped his arm. "Too right you're bad. That'll teach you to engage your brain next time before you open that big fat gob of yours."

"All right, there's no need to go on."

"And I'm glad you didn't use the nag word there."

"Jesus, you really do have your hand up your arse today, don'tcha?"

Katy glared at him. "No. Not at all. What about the two coppers who have sadly lost their lives, have the families been informed?"

"I believe so. It might be wise if you check on that, though."

"I'll do that now. Maybe they can fill in a few missing details for us, like why two coppers were on board the boat in the first place."

"It does seem odd," James agreed. "Oops, I forgot to tell you that the officers' boat was found drifting in the middle of the river a few miles or so that way."

Katy's gaze followed his pointed finger. "Hmm…it gets curiouser, doesn't it? Could they have fired the shot that hit the girl?"

"I doubt it. They have Tasers on them, no other weapons from what I can tell."

Katy scratched her neck. "What are we missing?"

"I don't think we are, not from what I can see. We just need to piece all the clues together. Once we find the weapon, I think that will answer a few of our puzzling questions."

"We'll see. Will you ring me with the results?"

"Of course. We'll pass all of our findings on to Patti, she'll be in touch with you within the next few days."

"Until then, we've got very little to go on. See you soon." Katy motioned for Charlie to follow her back to the car.

"Is that it?" Charlie asked once they were inside Katy's Ford Kuga.

"That's it. If we can't view the actual crime scene there's really no point in us hanging around. We could visit the mortuary, if you're up to it?"

Charlie's mouth twisted. "If we really have to. Does the smell linger on your clothes?"

Katy sniggered. "Sometimes, why?"

"It's a new suit."

"And very smart it is, too. You'll have protective clothing on. Best thing you can do is slip the scrubs on over your underwear, that way your clothes will keep all shiny and new."

"Good thinking. Sorry for sounding a wuss, it's just, I never spend much money on clothes and thought I'd push the boat out buying this to impress my new boss."

Katy laughed. "I'm sure DCI Roberts appreciated your efforts, too, Miss Simpkins."

"Actually, I was referring to you."

"Charlie! Stop it, you don't have to try and impress me. I know what genes you have running through you. They're from an impressive bloodline, what with your mother, and her father before her, being well-regarded in the Met."

"I know. Maybe that's just it, I don't want to feel as though I'm letting the side down by screwing up."

"You're an idiot. I have some advice for you."

Charlie frowned. "What's that?"

"Just be yourself. Yes, your name might have been the one thing that got your foot in the door in the first place, but since then, you've proven your worth in the K9 division enough for Sean to want you on his team. So, stop doubting your abilities. Hey, if you were a crap copper, there is no way on this earth you'd even be a passenger in this car, let alone be classed as my partner. You should be regarding that as an honour and a privilege. Oh God, that sounded so wrong. What I meant to say is…"

Charlie grinned. "I think I got your drift. Thanks for giving me a chance, Katy, it means the world to me to be here, working alongside my mother's best partner and good friend. I hope you don't regret having me."

"Stop with the negativity. Here's another piece of advice for you to consume: make sure you open your ears, don't let anything pass you by. Sometimes it's the snippet of information that comes your way which turns out to be the most vital piece of the puzzle in any investigation. I trust your integrity one hundred percent. Cards on the table, I wouldn't want anyone else as a partner."

Charlie's cheeks flushed. "I won't let you down, I promise."

"Damn right you won't, or I'll be straight on the phone to that mother of yours, forcing her out of retirement."

"Oh no, I don't think she'll ever consider coming back to the force now. She's settled really well up in Norfolk. She's living the dream as they say."

"Have you had the chance to visit her yet?"

"Briefly, Brandon and I made a flying visit a few weeks back to surprise her."

"I bet that went down well."

"Not really. She was up to her ankles in dog mess, hosing out the kennels. Ah, I remember those days well."

"Ah yes, of course, you used to run the rescue centre for her. You're a grafter, I'll give you that, Charlie."

"*Hard work never killed anyone* was one of my grandfather's favourite sayings."

"That's true enough." Katy slotted the car into gear and pulled away from the scene.

They arrived at the hospital fifteen minutes later and made their way down to the mortuary. One of Patti's assistants welcomed them.

"Hi, can I help?"

"We were hoping to join Patti, if it's not too late?"

"She's in the examination suite. I can ask for you."

"That'd be great. We'll wait here."

The woman walked the length of the corridor and entered a heavy door at the end. She emerged seconds later and motioned for them to join her.

She showed them into the locker room and pointed to the greens in the corner. "Help yourselves. When you're ready, go straight through, she's expecting you."

"Thanks."

The woman left, and Katy crossed the room to the cloth bag which held the green scrubs. "What size?"

"Either a small or maybe a medium would be better," Charlie replied, already stripping off her new suit and slipping it on one of the spare hangers sitting on the metal rail.

"Here you go. There should be a locker available, we'll put our personal belongings in there. Our clothes should be safe hanging up."

"I hope so, don't fancy going around wearing this all day back at the station."

"Yeah, I agree, hardly a fashion statement, are they? Good job AJ and Brandon aren't here to see us, it would kill our sex lives."

"You're not wrong."

Suited and booted in the non-high-fashion calf-style wellies, they ventured into the theatre.

Katy stopped at the door. "Are you sure you're up to this?"

"It's a part of the job I need to get used to ASAP, according to Mum."

"I don't think you ever get used to it, but yes, it's a necessary part of the job. I think Lorne's previous partner, Pete, always puked his way through the torture of being here."

"He was a funny sod. Nice guy, but funny all the same."

"I've heard some tales, I can tell you. Right, back to the task in hand. Be prepared, grab the pot of Vicks as soon as you get in there and slather it under your nostrils. Trust me, it'll help until you get used to the smell."

"You're not really selling it to me, boss."

Katy smiled and entered the room.

Patti paused talking to the recording machine and glanced their way. "Well, well, well, if we don't have yet another cracking Simpkins on our patch. Welcome, Charlie."

"Hi, Patti, Mum sends her regards."

"I need to give her a call. I'll do that later with an update on how you did during your first PM."

Katy wagged her finger at the pathologist. "Leave the poor girl alone, give her a bloody chance, Patti."

"I'm teasing. You'll be fine. You come from the best stock around. That's good enough for me. I have confidence in you, Charlie."

"Thanks, I hope I don't let you down."

Katy handed Charlie the pot of Vicks and showed her how much to use of the slippery, smelly product.

Charlie heaved at the odour. "I'm not sure which is worse." She nodded at the corpse where the Y-section had been made and the innards were on view.

"It would be better if you could do without," Patti advised.

"I think I'll give it a go."

Katy placed the jar back on the stainless-steel trolley. "Well, I bloody need it, and no one is going to persuade me otherwise. On your head be it, Charlie."

"I'll risk it."

"Right, what have we got?" Katy asked, glancing down the length of the corpse's charred remains.

"I've already established the man had his throat cut. That was before the fire took place as the wounds are singed."

"Okay, have you managed to ID him yet?"

"No, not yet. He was in a bathing suit, few places possible to store any form of ID as you can imagine." Patti held up a clear evidence bag, holding up the remains of a charred pair of fluorescent-green budgie smugglers.

Katy cringed. "Nice taste in beach attire, I don't think."

"I won't be rushing out to buy any for Brandon, that's for sure," Charlie chipped in.

"If you two have quite finished dissing the man's fashion endeavours. As I was saying, his throat was cut. He also suffered a broken jaw. Now, whether that was caused during the accident, I'm not too sure. There are also a number of contusions around his face, again, similar outcome, I'm just not sure when they happened."

"It's all a damn mystery," Katy muttered. "Have you had a chance to do the PMs on the other victims yet?"

"No, he's my first. Sorry for the loss of your two colleagues. I'll do my very best to get the results back to you quickly. I've already had a call from their boss, demanding the results ASAP. He was on his way to inform the families."

"Tough job. I hate doing it. I'll have that pleasure to come when we ID the other victim."

"I don't envy you. All right if I proceed?" Patti asked.

"Go for it."

She ran through any nicks or extra bruising she found on the corpse and then moved on to remove the organs. "His liver is pickled, a heavy drinker for sure."

"Goes with the territory, if it's who we perceive him to be. James, the head technician at the scene, said he was likely Ray Thatcham, a local businessman. The boat was registered in his name."

"Okay, in that case, you know more than me for a change." Patti removed his heart and prodded it. "Again, signs of a rich diet, fatty tissue surrounding the heart here and here." She poked at two separate areas.

"Sounds about right."

The rest of the post-mortem was carried out swiftly with no further conclusions of note.

"That's about it. I'm going to patch him up the best I can. I can categorically say that the wound to his throat was the fatal blow that ended his, what would appear to have been, extravagant lifestyle."

"Sounds plausible to me. Hang on, I've just thought of something. James said the gent was all over Google."

"We can match any photos that are on the internet, if that's what you're saying? His face isn't too charred. I took some photos of him before I started the PM."

Patti crossed the room and returned with her camera. She showed Katy the photos she'd snapped off. "It'll have to do. I'll get them sent to your phone when I'm back in my office. I'm going to take a break after I've finished here, before I start on the next one."

"Great stuff. We'll get changed."

"I'll be another fifteen to twenty minutes on this one, can you hang around?"

"Of course. It's not like we have anything else to go on."

2

After successfully obtaining an ID for the man, Katy rang the station and asked Karen to find an address for the victim. She'd rung them back almost instantly, and now they were en route to break the news to the man's family.

"Damn, I could do with your mum's input for this one. I detest with a capital D this part."

"Surprisingly enough, Mum used to say the same."

"Wow, you've shocked me there. She always came across so calm and collected with the right amount of empathy chucked in for good measure. You learn something new every day, I guess. Feel free to take over this side of things once you've settled in more, won't you?"

Charlie grimaced. "I'd rather leave the onerous chore up to you, thanks all the same."

"Yeah, I had a feeling that was going to be your response. Maybe we should stop off and have a quick drink on the way, to give me some Dutch courage."

Charlie stared at her. "Are you talking alcohol or caffeine?"

"Don't tempt me. Maybe caffeine would be the better option, a bacon sarnie wouldn't go amiss either. What say you?"

Her partner's tummy grumbled, giving Katy her answer. Charlie glanced down at her stomach and said, "Traitor. All right, it does sound tempting."

Katy pulled into a greasy spoon café she'd heard good things about in the area, and they sat there for half an hour, discussing the case and its different scenarios over a coffee and a calorie-laden bacon roll. Then they got on the road again.

Charlie rubbed her tummy. "I've eaten too much. Don't be surprised if I fall asleep during the afternoon shift."

Katy puffed out her cheeks. "Funny that, I was just thinking the same. I doubt if I'll need any dinner this evening. Worth it, though, eh?"

"It was. I hope that's not going to become a regular thing. I'll be ten stone heavier in no time at all working alongside you."

"Maybe a once-a-month treat, how does that sound?"

"It would be better if you'd said once every six months."

Katy sniggered. "You're young enough to work it off, unlike me."

Charlie tutted. "Bloody hell, you're hardly past it, what are you, thirty-three?"

"Not far off. Actually, I'm thirty-two."

"And you think that's old?"

"All right, maybe I was stretching the truth a little. I feel old some days, especially when Georgina hasn't slept well."

"The joys of having kids. AJ is definitely a one-off. Not sure any bloke I know would be prepared to give up his job to care for his child."

"He is that. Never complains either, which is a blessing. Right, we're getting closer now. Another few miles and we should be there."

"The houses in this area must cost a bob or two."

"Not short of Mayfair prices, last I heard."

Katy approached the house cautiously. The tall wrought iron gates were locked, and there was an intercom halfway up the gatepost pillar. Katy exited the car and pressed the buzzer.

"Yes." A man's voice filtered through the grill.

"Hi, I'm DI Katy Foster. Is Mrs Thatcham at home, please?"

"She is. Just a moment, I'll see if she has the time to see you. May I ask what it's regarding?"

"It's a personal issue."

"Very well. I'll be back soon."

Katy stood upright and tilted her head towards the sun which had suddenly made an appearance through the heavy grey clouds.

The gates opened, and Katy ran back to the car to drive through them in case they were on some kind of timer and closed before she had the chance to enter.

Charlie whistled as they turned the corner of the sweeping drive. "Christ, this place is ginormous."

"And some," Katy agreed. "Worth a heap of money, too. He must have been really successful."

"Either that or he was bent," Charlie added.

They left the car and made their way across the drive, their heels sinking into the deep gravel. "You could have something there. Let's see what the wife has to say."

A man in a dark suit held the large double front doors open for them.

Katy and Charlie flashed their warrant cards. He nodded and motioned for them to follow him. They walked across the bright, polished white marble floor up a wide hallway to the rear of the property. The living room had a glass wall which overlooked the colourful garden and the fields beyond. The view took Katy's breath away. She was so drawn by it that she neglected to see the smartly dressed woman seated at a mahogany desk at the other end of the huge room until the man pointed her out.

"Mrs Thatcham. Is there anything else, ma'am?"

"No, Donald. I don't think so. Come closer, ladies."

Katy smiled as she approached the woman with Charlie. "I'm DI Katy Foster, and this is my partner, DC Charlie Simpkins."

"How quaint. Is that short for Charlotte or Charlene?"

Charlie smiled. "Charlene, I loathe it. Not sure what my parents were thinking when they named me."

"We all have our crosses to bear. My middle name is Enid, go figure. Anyway, what brings the police to my door at this time of the day?"

"We're following up on a general enquiry regarding your husband."

Mrs Thatcham turned in her seat and crossed her long legs, the slit in her dress falling to one side, her tan accentuating her shapely pins. "Oh my, what's Ray been up to now?"

"Perhaps you can tell us when you last saw your husband?" Katy asked.

"Yesterday morning. He was away overnight on a business meeting."

"I see. May I ask where?"

"In the city. I know, why stay overnight when you live in the same city, right? Well, he was involved in a very important meeting and entertaining an influential client. He felt it would be better staying in a hotel overnight, especially with the amount of drink that would be consumed during the evening."

"And you haven't had any form of contact with him since?"

"No. That's what I said. What's going on here?"

"The client, were they male or female?"

"Male. Are you going to answer me? I asked you what this is all about."

"Does your husband own a boat, Mrs Thatcham?"

"Yes, why?"

"And where is it usually moored?"

"In Sunbury-on-Thames." She unfolded her legs and stood. "I'm not liking where these questions are leading. I must insist you get to the point and tell me why you're here."

"Maybe you should sit down again for what I have to tell you."

"And maybe you should stop wasting my time and get on with it."

"Okay, if that's what you want. It is with regret that I have to tell you we believe your husband died in an incident…"

Mrs Thatcham screamed. A scream which appeared to echo around the room, out into the hallway and back again. "What? This can't be true."

Donald reappeared in the doorway. "Is everything all right, ma'am?"

"No, it's not. Get me a large whisky and be quick about it, man."

"Very well. Right away, ma'am." He returned sharpish with a cut-glass tumbler half-filled with amber liquid.

Mrs Thatcham snatched the glass from his hand and downed the contents in two gulps, then she slipped into her seat again, placed her elbows on the desk and supported her head. "I can't believe this. How?"

"We believe it could have been a boating incident, although there is reason to believe your husband was murdered."

"What? In a boating incident? How is that possible?"

Katy peered over her shoulder at the couch. "May we take a seat?"

"Of course. Sorry."

"No need to apologise," Katy replied.

Charlie withdrew her notebook.

"Our investigation is in its infancy at present, so I doubt if we'll be able to answer most of your questions. What I can tell you is, there were three other people killed at the same time. Two police officers and a female."

Mrs Thatcham scratched her head and frowned. "Female? None of this is making sense. Are you sure it's him?"

"We've just come from the mortuary. We have a photo, it's not pleasant, we used that to match against his internet persona. If that makes sense."

"Not really. Show me the picture."

"I'm not sure I should do that. You'll be asked to make a formal ID when the time is right."

"Then I refuse to acknowledge that he's dead. I'm going to ring him." She picked up her mobile and tapped in a password then held the phone to her ear. When it rang and remained unanswered, she slammed it down and screamed again.

Katy stared at Charlie unsure how to proceed. Eventually, she cleared her throat and asked, "Did he tell you which hotel he was staying at last night? Maybe we could check with them."

Mrs Thatcham nodded, scrolled through her contacts, and then placed the phone to her ear. "Yes, this is Paula Thatcham, did my husband stay there last night?" Her expression clouded over. "I see, and when was the last time you saw him?" She stared at the wall in front of her then hung up.

"I take it it's not good news?" Katy probed.

"No. He hasn't been seen there for several months."

"And that has come as a surprise to you?"

"Yes, he has regular overnight meetings and has told me in the past that he always stays at the same hotel as it's just around the corner from his office. The lying, cheating…no-good fucking waste of space."

Katy raised a hand. "I'm sorry, it wouldn't be fair to go down that route, not yet."

"But you told me there was a woman on board *our* boat. What were the two coppers doing there? Was it some kind of orgy or what?"

"No, I think you're way off the mark there. We've yet to speak to the control centre to find out what went on."

"Did your lot kill him? It was only a matter of time."

Katy tilted her head and asked, "Why would you say that? Has your husband been in trouble with the police before?"

Paula fell silent, her focus remaining on the blank wall beside her.

"Paula?" Katy prompted.

"What? I'm not saying another word. I know your lot, you'll twist everything I say to suit your means."

"By that, am I to believe your husband has been in trouble with the police in the past then?"

"Might have been. That's all I'm saying. If you want to know more, I suggest you look at your records. Most of them are fake anyway, just remember that, won't you?"

"I'm giving you a chance to give your side of the story. That's if you're willing."

"I'm not. I've said more than enough. Tell me when I can see my husband."

"The pathologist will call you to make the arrangements. I haven't quite finished asking my questions, if you'll just give us a few minutes more?"

Paula folded her arms and glared at Katy. "Go on. Make it quick."

Katy recognised that her mood had changed from grieving widow to feisty wife. She was guessing the woman's answers would be few and far between, judging by her expression and manner, but she was willing to give it a go. "Perhaps you can fill us in a little on your husband's background."

"Meaning?"

"What type of business did he own?"

"An import and export business."

"How many years has he owned it?"

"Fifteen, give or take a year or two. I don't know, my head is elsewhere right now. Like wondering what a woman was doing on my damn boat with my husband and why four people, including a couple of sodding coppers, are dead and you're sitting here asking me about his bloody business."

"I'm sorry, it could be important."

"How?"

"Perhaps he's done something wrong businesswise lately which could have resulted in his death."

"Are you for real, lady?"

"It's a genuine observation. Would you say your husband's business is a legitimate one?"

"Yes," she answered and abruptly fell silent again.

Katy got the distinct impression that Paula Thatcham wasn't being completely truthful with her.

"Mrs Thatcham, if you know something it would be better if you confided in us."

"Or else what?"

"It wasn't a threat, I'm sorry if it sounded that way."

Paula heaved out a sigh. "Well, that would make a bloody change around here. Are you going to be long? I have a client due in half an hour and I need to prepare a few samples for them."

"May I ask what you do?"

Paula threw her arm out and cast it around the room. "Can't you tell? I'm an interior designer to the rich and famous."

"I see. Yes, you've definitely got a discerning eye, I'll give you that."

"That sounded like you just delivered an insult."

Katy gasped. "Did it? That's the complete opposite to how it should've come across. Forgive me. Please, if there's anything that has gone on in your husband's recent past that we should know about, it would be better if you told us now rather than a few days down the line."

"There isn't, not that I know of. What about the bitch who was with him, do you know who she was? Maybe she had a husband and he found out they were having an affair and decided to bump the pair of them off."

"Was your husband prone to having a wandering eye?"

"Years ago, yes. I thought we'd got past that. Shows how much I know, doesn't it?"

"Is it likely that someone at his firm might know who the woman is?"

"How the dickens should I know? You'll have to ask them, if they'll tell you the truth, that is."

"Any reason why they shouldn't?"

"Depends how long he'd been seeing the bitch behind my back. Someone at that place would have known about it. I'm gutted."

"His death must have come as a great shock."

"No, I mean, I'm gutted I never got the chance to fucking kill the bastard myself."

"I don't believe you would have harmed him."

"Are you saying I'm all mouth and no action? I can assure you, it wouldn't be the first time I'd have battered him to within an inch of his life. That's one thing I wouldn't have put up with, he knew that. He must have had a death wish. The bastard. How could he ruin the memories I have of him now that he's gone? He knew how much I abhorred the thought of him sticking his dick in someone else's hole and then coming home to me. No woman should have to live through that."

Despite her posh façade, the woman's fishwife tongue was getting the better of her.

"I agree. If he was aware of how you felt, why do you think he was with another woman?"

"How the sodding hell should I know?"

"Did he have a best friend, someone he might have confided in perhaps?"

Her eyes narrowed as she thought. "Maybe Dan would know. I'll ring him."

Katy held a hand up, preventing Paula from reaching for her phone. "I think we should be the ones to tackle him. Do you have his number or address?"

"He works at Enright Towers with Ray, at least he used to. I need to speak to him as well, so tell him to get in touch when you eventually track him down."

"We will. We'll call and see him next. What about around here, have you had any bother from anyone in the past few months?"

"No. I can't think of anything out of the ordinary. If he was in any kind of trouble, I think he would have said something. However, saying that, I'm not sure he would have after what you've told me. And to think, I thought I knew him well. Why? Why was he cheating on me? I can't believe he'd do it. We had a good sex life, and I thought we were happy, and now I find out he's had someone on the side. I'm reeling from that news."

"Please, we don't know why the woman was there. I wouldn't dwell on it, not until all the facts come out."

"If I find out Dan knew, I'll bloody kill him. I had a right to know he was cheating, if he was. Shit! Why isn't the bastard around for me to ask him? I'll never get the answers I want now."

Katy sighed. The woman was rambling all of a sudden, something she couldn't abide. "Are you sure there's nothing else you think we should know?"

"No, I've told you. I'm going to ask you to leave now. I need to get my head straight before my client arrives."

Katy and Charlie stood. "We understand. Thank you for giving us some of your valuable time today. We're sorry for your loss."

"Thanks. I'll show you to the door."

Outside the house, Katy said, "Damn, I didn't handle that very well, did I?"

"Nonsense. Everything was going well until you mentioned the other woman. I think I would've reacted the same way she had if I heard that bolt out of the blue. You shouldn't blame yourself."

"Thanks, I think you're being kind, though. Never mind, it's done and dusted, I can't take the words back."

Charlie remained quiet until they were back inside the car. "Saying that, I kind of got the impression that she was keeping something from us, didn't you?"

"I'm not sure. If I'm honest with you, I was too damned focussed on trying not to put my foot in it to notice. But if that's what your intuition is telling you then I'm prepared to go along with that. You think her husband was importing illegal stuff? Drugs or possibly people trafficking?"

"It could be anything judging by the cost of this place. You've got to be looking at around twenty-five million for this gaff. How many legit companies do you know that would bring in that amount?"

"You've got a point. Okay, let's call in at his office and see for ourselves."

3

*K*aty parked in the underground car park and locked the vehicle. They rode the swanky lift up to the top floor of Enright Towers and approached the receptionist.

Katy flashed her warrant card. "Hi, DI Katy Foster and DC Charlie Simpkins. We're here to speak with Ray Thatcham's partner, Dan... sorry, I don't have his surname."

"That's no problem, it's Williams. He's bound to ask me what this is about, what shall I tell him?"

"It's about a colleague. Thanks." Katy decided to keep her answer brief and simple.

The receptionist left her desk, and this gave Katy and Charlie the chance to survey the area.

"Pretty swish. It obviously costs a packet to run this place, especially as it's situated in the heart of the city. I'm not getting good vibes about this, are you?"

Charlie shook her head. "Do you think we should call for backup?"

"No, however, I think we should be guarded in what we say and do, okay?"

"I'll follow your lead on that one, boss."

The receptionist reappeared and asked them to follow her down a

wide carpeted hallway and into an office with one of the most spectac-
ular views of London Katy had ever seen. She hid her awe well and
remained focussed on the task in hand.

Dan Williams leapt out of his chair and raced around his desk to
shake their hands, a little too enthusiastically for Katy's liking.

"Hello, sir. We appreciate you taking time out of your busy
schedule to speak with us today."

"Sandy mentioned your visit was concerning a colleague. May I
ask who? Please, take a seat." He returned and sat behind his desk and
immediately picked up a pen which he clicked to an unknown tune.

"Your partner, Ray Thatcham." Katy said the man's name in case
there were several partners in the firm. At this point, they just weren't
sure how things were run around here.

"I see. What about Ray? Wait, let me stop you there. The last I
heard from him was first thing yesterday morning. I've tried at regular
intervals to contact him about a pressing issue since yesterday afternoon, and my success has been limited. When I say limited, what I
really meant was non-existent. Is something wrong? Is that why you're
here?"

"Where did he tell you he was going?"

The man's gaze darted between Katy and Charlie, and then his
brow furrowed. He appeared to shuffle uncomfortably, squirming, to be
exact. "He, well, he...umm...how do I put this?"

"The truth would be a good idea, Dan, thanks."

"Why? What's he done?"

"I'll answer that when you tell me what your partner was up to
yesterday, because according to Paula, his wife, he was supposed to be
away on business at a local hotel."

"Ah, yes, he was. No, he wasn't, I mean...that's what he wanted
her to know."

"What are you trying to tell us? I'm struggling to decipher it right
now."

He flung himself back in the chair and threw the pen on the desk.
"All right, you've forced it out of me. He's having an affair with one of
the new girls, Tina Lascombe."

"New girls, as in, she works alongside him?"

"Yes, as a secretary. She's a stand-in for Susan who is on maternity leave. She's due back in a week or so, therefore, Ray decided to play hookie with Tina, to show how appreciative of her work he was."

"By sleeping with her behind his wife's back, is that what you're hinting at?"

"Yes. Look, he's one of those men who has certain urges which need satisfying."

"Behind his wife's back?" Katy had pleasure in repeating to get her point across.

"If you like, yes."

"Does he have any kids?"

"Yes, the twins. Evie and Jessie attend private school."

"So they're out of the way, is that it?" Katy neither liked nor respected this man or his partner, the dead victim. "Why get married in the first place if all he really wants to do is fool around with younger women? Sorry, that's me being presumptuous. How old is Miss Lascombe?"

He chewed his lip for a second as if debating her question. "Twenty-three, I believe."

"Hmm…all right, thanks for that information, it'll come in handy for our investigation."

"Which is? You haven't really told me what all this is about, have you?"

Ignoring his question, Katy pressed on. "Did Ray say where he would be taking Miss Lascombe for the day?"

"Out on his boat. She's new, and he wanted to impress the girl."

"Any reason he felt the need to impress her when he owns one of the biggest companies in London? That's my assumption by the way, not the facts speaking."

"No, you're right. It's a male thing. Yes, we're a highly successful firm, you've hit the nail on the head there. He's always been one for the ladies, that one."

Katy sighed and puffed out her cheeks. "Fair enough, and yet his wife is in the dark about this affair and likely the numerous liaisons he's had before Miss Lascombe, is that what you're expecting me to believe?"

He sat upright again. "I don't understand what any of this has to do with you coming here today. Please either state your business or return at a later date when Ray is around to answer your questions directly regarding his personal life, which really has nothing to do with me."

"Oh, I'm sure it has everything to do with you, when two members of your team decide to go off for the day together, but maybe that's my take on things. Okay, here's why we're visiting you today. Yesterday afternoon, Ray Thatcham and who we now believe to be Tina Lascombe, died on board his boat."

"*What*? Is this some kind of warped wind-up?"

"Sadly not. Miss Lascombe is yet to be formally identified, but given what you've just told us, I think we can safely say the other victim was her."

He sat there in silence, shaking his head slowly for a while, an ashen hue filling his cheeks.

Katy was growing concerned by his demeanour and asked, "Are you okay, Dan?"

"I'm devastated. How the hell...? What in the...? God, I can't believe what you've just told me. Dead? How can they both be dead? What happened?"

"Before I reveal that, perhaps you wouldn't mind telling me what line of business you're in, by that I mean, what do you export and import?"

A twinkle glinted in his eye. "Goods."

"That doesn't really tell me a lot. What goods? And where do you import and export to and from?"

"All over the world."

Katy's chest burned with frustration. It was obvious the man was being deliberately evasive, why?

"If that's the way you want to play things, I'll have no other option than to get a warrant to search the premises and take an in-depth look into your accounts, is that what you want, sir?"

"Do what you like, although I have to say that's a little extreme considering what you've told me, that Ray and Tina died in a boating accident."

"I don't remember telling you that." She turned to face her partner. "Did I say that, DC Simpkins?"

"Nope, you said nothing of the sort," Charlie backed her up.

His frown returned. "You said they died on board the boat. All right, maybe I presumed it was an accident. So, what are you telling me then?"

"Sir, we're here to obtain answers in a murder investigation."

"What the…? No way! Who the fuck…? Sorry. Why would anyone want to kill Ray?" He left his desk and went to stand by the window with its view of all the tourist attractions on offer in the city. "Jesus, I can't get my head around this. How?"

Katy shrugged when he peered over his shoulder. "I can't go into detail, although I can tell you that they weren't the only two people to have lost their lives on the boat."

He turned and folded his arms. "What are you saying? Who else died?"

"Two police officers. Now, do you understand the necessity for our being here, asking these questions?"

"Fuck! Two coppers, and this all took place on the boat, you say?"

"That's correct. Do you have an explanation for that?"

His flattened hand slammed against his chest. "Me? Why should I? This is all news to me. Listen here, I'm not sure what you're bloody insinuating by coming here, but I can assure you, you're bloody barking up the wrong tree thinking you can bully me into answering your damn questions. You hear me? Either state what you want or fuck off. Yes, I could have possibly said that more politely, but to be honest with you, you're coming across as though you think I had something to do with this shit. I can categorically deny it and I'd be willing to pay for a top barrister to wipe the floor with you if you insist on taking this further."

"First of all, you might want to calm down a bit, sir. All I'm doing is trying to get some background information on your business partner.

Secondly, you're acting as though I've hit a nerve and you're doing your best to punish me verbally for achieving that."

He slumped into his chair again and mumbled an apology. "I didn't mean to fly off the handle, this news is crucifying me, you have to understand that. Ray wasn't just my business partner, he was like a brother to me."

"If you were that close, perhaps you wouldn't mind telling us the nature of your business?" Katy tried once more.

"I've told you. I wish you'd stop hounding me on that."

"I'm sorry if you think that's what I'm doing. I'm sure you can understand the need to try and ascertain if Ray had any dodgy dealings in his past."

"I can't. Are you telling me that your mob killed him?"

"No, at this stage in the investigation, we're unsure how or why four people died aboard that boat. The fact is they did, and all four of them appeared to have been murdered during the trip."

"How is that possible? Did your lot strike first? Kill Ray and Tina and then kill themselves?" His expression was one of puzzlement as he said the words out loud. "That doesn't make any sense, does it?"

"No, you're right, it doesn't make sense at all. Which is why we have to deal with the facts and ask why you think the police might have boarded the vessel in the first place."

He held his hands out to the side. "As if I'd know that. Can't you ask that internally?"

"We're going to. I'm sure it's all going to come back to my first question: what do you import and export, sir?"

"Jesus, you do like to keep repeating yourself, don't you? Is this your way of trying to obtain the truth? By wearing me down? Is that it?"

"Not at all. As I've already stated, if you're not prepared to be open and truthful then I'll have no hesitation in obtaining a warrant for Ray's home and business address."

He shrugged. "Then tootle off and do it because I ain't about to divulge any of my contacts or business dealings with the likes of you. For all I know, you could be here under false pretences to obtain the information so that you can pass it on to one of my competitors."

"Why would I do that, sir?"

"It's well known the police operate mostly on backhanders."

Katy resisted the temptation to laugh. "Is that right? Not these two coppers, I can assure you. We're whiter than a snow drift in New Mexico and can't abide dodgy coppers."

"Well, that makes a frigging change. Mind you, in my experience, those who spout their innocence are usually more corrupt than those who keep schtum."

"Really? We'll have to agree to differ on that one then, won't we?"

"We will. Now, if you don't mind, I'd like to get on with my day, it's now got a lot tougher after the news you've just delivered."

"I haven't finished yet, if it's all the same to you."

He heaved out an exasperated breath and reclined in his chair. "Go on, get on with it then."

"I'd like to know if Ray has mentioned being worried or concerned about anything either in his business or personal life in the past few weeks."

"No, nothing at all. He was a happy-go-lucky kind of chap. Who worked his nuts off to get this business off the ground, we both did. Now it's thriving, and I'm left to man the ship alone. I just hope it doesn't hit an iceberg and frigging sink. I have a lot of money tied up in it that I wouldn't mind hanging on to."

"How did the business begin? And how long ago did you start up?"

"Around fifteen years ago. Ray and I have been friends for years, met each other in our teens. Found out we had the same philosophy in life."

"Which was?"

"To work hard and reap the benefits as a reward for all our hard work and the excessive hours we needed to put into a venture."

"Why go into the import and export trade?"

"It seemed a good idea at the time."

"It's obviously paid off for you, judging by this building and Ray's mansion, which we visited earlier."

"My God, how did Paula take the news?"

"About her husband's death? She was understandably upset."

His eyes widened. "Don't tell me you mentioned Tina to her?"

"We did, we had to. We had no idea who the woman was and we were trying to obtain an ID for her."

"Shit! I bet she went ballistic, didn't she?"

"She was determined to ring you while we were there. We managed to persuade her not to. No doubt she'll be in touch with you soon, though."

"Fucking hell! What am I going to tell her? Jesus, why did this shit have to land on my doorstep at a time like this?"

"Time like this?" Katy inclined her head to ask.

"My father is seriously ill. I've had to take my eye off the ball around here in the past few weeks to care for him and my mum."

"I'm sorry to hear that. What's wrong with him?"

"He's scheduled to have a triple bypass within the next couple of weeks. He's getting weaker by the day. Mum reckons he's not going to make it."

"My father had a heart problem a few years back so I sympathise with you. Surely, if you're wealthy, can't you afford to go private?"

"Dad's a stickler, he's insisting we go through the NHS. I know, Mum and I have been trying our best to make him see sense. All he keeps saying is that if his time is up then so be it."

"Oh dear, sorry to hear that. Men can be stubborn in the extreme at times."

"Yep, I can't argue with you there."

"Going back to Ray, please try and think if he's been under any form of pressure from anyone lately."

"Businesswise, is that what you're suggesting?"

"Yes, or in his personal life?"

His mouth turned down at the sides, and he shook his head. "I can't think of anything at all."

"All right, what about Tina, what can you tell us about her?"

"She showed up as a temp sometime last year and come and gone a few times since, and Ray took an instant liking to her. He persuaded her to stay on when one of the other secretaries, not Susan, left to move north with her family. Her husband got relocated with his job."

"Did Tina have a partner or was she single?"

"I'm not sure. I've always presumed she was single. She chased Ray as much as he chased her, if you get my drift?"

"I do. Would you mind getting her personnel file for us, if you possess one?"

"Sure. It's in the other office. I'll be right back." He wheeled back his chair and dived out of the room only to return a few minutes later with a manila folder which he handed to Katy.

"Take this address down, DC Simpkins, will you? Seventeen Cheadle Road. According to this she isn't married. Her next of kin is listed as her mother, Margaret Lascombe. Her phone number is…" She showed Charlie the number to jot down. "We'll try and contact her after we leave here. There's no address for her on file. We'll ring and see where she's located." Katy placed the file on the desk and slid it back to Dan. "Thanks, it's a start anyway. Are you sure you don't want to divulge more about your business, sir? It'll save a lot of hassle in the long run."

"I'm sure. As far as I'm concerned, everything is above board around here. You can still earn a lot of money through a legitimate business, you know, Inspector."

Katy smiled. "Okay, we'll still need to seek a warrant, all the same. Right, if there's nothing else you wish to add, we'll get going." She rose from her seat, and Charlie followed her to the door. "We'll let you know when we obtain the warrant."

"You do that." He smiled tautly and dismissed her by reaching for the phone on his desk.

On the way down in the lift, Katy expelled a breath. "Well, that proved pretty pointless."

Charlie stared up at the lights as they descended. "At least we found out who the woman was and we can do something about that."

"Yeah, another trip to a bloody relative. Joy of joys. I wish I could fob off this part of the job onto someone else."

"I can understand your reluctance. Maybe the mother will be able to fill in some gaps for us."

"Possibly." Katy called the woman and obtained her address. "It's going to take us around twenty minutes to get there. Can you ring Thames Valley Police for me, see what the story is there?"

"Sure." Charlie fished out her phone and looked up the number. "Shall I put it on speaker?"

"Yep, beats listening to Take That on Smooth all the time." Katy grinned.

They ended up getting all the information they needed from Sergeant Davidson who took the call.

"So, they were called to the scene because of a disturbance?" Katy summarised.

"That's correct," Davidson said. "There were four people on board the boat when they received the call."

"Four? How strange. Well, it is in one respect, however, it certainly clears things up. We were struggling to make sense of who killed whom. Thanks for taking the time to speak to us, sending our condolences to your colleagues' families."

"Thanks, I'll pass that on. Give me a shout if you need any further information."

"We'll do that."

Charlie ended the call. "How the hell did the other two get off the boat then?"

"Maybe it didn't go up in flames until they'd left the boat."

Charlie's nod gained momentum. "You could be right. They set the fire in the hope it would cover their tracks. They nearly succeeded as well. Surely someone saw something down there. Do you think we should ask for help from the general public?"

"It might be an idea. Let's get this onerous task out of the way first and then reassess things."

The house they were after was situated in the middle of a snug row of terraced houses with dozens of cars littering the road. Katy parked in the only slot available at the end of a block of vehicles, and they walked back to the house.

Katy rang the bell. It was answered almost instantaneously by a smartly dressed woman in her late fifties, who was chatting to someone on her mobile.

"All right, Nadine, I've gotta go, there's someone standing on my doorstep. We'll meet up for lunch as soon as I have a spare five minutes, I promise. Love you lots." She pushed the button to end the call and smiled. "Hello, sorry about that. Can I help?"

Katy and Charlie produced their IDs, and Katy introduced them, "Mrs Lascombe. I called earlier. Is it all right if we come in to speak with you for a few minutes?"

"You did, you hung up before I got the chance to ask you what this is all about?" She glanced over Katy's shoulder and waved at a passerby.

"Your daughter, Tina."

"What? She's not home right now. She's away for a few days."

"It would be better inside," Katy pressed, already feeling agitated about how she would tell the woman the heartbreaking news.

"Very well, I haven't got long, though. I have an appointment with my gynaecologist in an hour and I'll need to get public transport to the hospital, and we all know how unreliable that can be."

"It's fine. We won't keep you long."

Mrs Lascombe led them into an immaculately presented lounge. No clutter and nothing out of place from what Katy could tell, a stark contrast to her own home which was littered with Georgina's toys, despite AJ's best efforts to keep the place tidy.

"Take a seat. Now, what's this about Tina?"

Katy and Charlie sat on the couch while the woman lowered herself into a tartan-covered armchair by the window.

"When was the last time you heard from your daughter?"

"I last spoke and saw her the day before yesterday. She packed a bag and told me she was spending a few days with her fella. I didn't ask where, she's a grown woman. Why? Has she done something wrong?"

"Can you tell us what you know about her boyfriend?"

She rolled her eyes. "Her *married* boyfriend, you mean. It was a bit of a sore point between us. She assured me she knew what she was doing, the risks she was taking, and to stop nagging her. I agreed. I hated that she was carrying on behind his wife's back. You know what young girls are like, though. Apparently he promised her the earth and she fell for it."

"Have they been seeing each other very long?"

"A few months, I suppose. What's with all the questions? Has my daughter done something against the law, is that why you're here?"

Katy prepared herself and tried to steady her breathing. "It's with regret I have to inform you that yesterday afternoon a woman who we believe to be your daughter lost her life in an incident we're investigating."

Mrs Lascombe sat perfectly still, stunned. Slowly, as the news sank in, she shook her head as if rejecting the unwanted news. She whispered, "No, this can't be happening. I need to ring her." She tapped a number into the mobile she was holding and stared at Katy while it rang out. Tears dripped onto her cheeks as the realisation dawned on her. "How? Was she with him? Did he kill her?"

"What makes you say that?"

She shrugged. "Nothing good could have come out of the situation, could it?"

"If you're asking us if he killed her, we can't answer that just yet. If it's any consolation, she didn't die alone."

"Oh right. Did he die as well?"

"Yes. He was murdered. We're unsure, at present, what the cause of death will be for who we assume to be your daughter."

Her brow pinched into tight wrinkles. "What's that supposed to mean?"

"We're trying to piece together what happened. It's going to be difficult, and the crime scene analysis will be hampered somewhat because there was a fire on board the boat."

"Boat? What boat? Where? Here in the UK, or are you telling me this happened abroad somewhere? I'm confused, please, can't you tell me outright how this happened?"

"As far as we know, Tina and her boss—you're aware she was

seeing her boss, aren't you?" Katy asked, cringing when she thought she'd put her foot in it.

"Yes, that's why I had a go at her. It's not right that these men should be allowed to take advantage of the women who work for them. They dangle all sorts of promises for them to grasp. Despicable, especially when he was bloody married. You know what young girls are like, they think they know best, and now…she's gone. What the hell does that say about my mothering skills? If only I had spoken to her as an equal, maybe I could have persuaded her not to get involved with the bastard. Sorry for speaking ill of the dead, but this is my daughter we're talking about here. My only child."

"I'm sorry for your loss. Maybe you can tell us more about their relationship, if you wouldn't mind?"

"What's to tell? He set his sights on my beautiful baby, and the rest is history. He splashed the cash around, she fluttered her eyelashes, and he promised her the earth."

Katy's interest went up a notch. "Do you think he was planning on leaving his wife for your daughter?"

"Are you suggesting she might be behind their deaths?"

"Not outright, no. However, we'll definitely be looking into that side of things during our investigation."

"You think a woman would be capable of such an act?"

"Who knows, if the risks are high and she has everything to lose if he ditches her?"

"Hard to fathom, but nothing should surprise me any more in this cruel world. I don't think the news has sunk in yet. Why am I not devastated? I should be, shouldn't I?"

"Grief presents itself in different ways. Because we haven't got a formal identification yet, you still have hope. Maybe when we're gone it will sink in and hit you. Do you want me to ring anyone, maybe get someone over here to sit with you?"

"No. I think I'll be all right. If I sense I can't cope after you've gone, I'll call someone. Damn, what about my hospital appointment? I've waited over a year to get one. They think I have cancer. I'm about to get the prognosis today." Her head bowed, and she clenched her fists in her lap. "I could have done with Tina's support today, but she chose to be with him."

"I'm sorry to hear that. Would you like us to give you a lift rather than you relying on public transport?"

"That's very kind of you, but I'll pass. I'd rather go alone, it'll give me time to think. Oh gosh, how on earth do you start planning your daughter's funeral? Where do I begin if it is her?"

"There are grief counsellors out there willing to help you. Would you like me to give you a number you can ring?"

"No. I don't think I can deal with it right now. Let me work through the process first. At least, that's what I think I need to do. Who knows? My God, what am I bloody saying? She's possibly dead, and I'm sitting here numb, not thinking straight. What is wrong with me?"

"Please, don't beat yourself up about this," Katy said, suddenly out of her depth, not knowing what to say next to heap yet more sympathy on the woman.

"Why don't I make you a drink?" Charlie offered.

"Yes, maybe that would be a good idea," Mrs Lascombe replied. "Tea, milk, two sugars. Thank you, dear."

"Nothing for me, Charlie," Katy chipped in.

While Charlie was out of the room, Katy tried to speak to the woman. Her aim wasn't to bombard her with questions but to lend her a sympathetic ear. "If you need to talk about Tina, feel free. Is her father around?"

"No. He walked out on us when I was eight months pregnant. Haven't seen or heard from the bastard since then either."

"That's disgusting. I'm so sorry."

"Don't be. We've coped better without him. He was a druggie and an alcoholic who beat the shit out of me most days. I'm surprised Tina wasn't born with any defects, the number of times he either punched or kicked me in the stomach, trying to make me have a miscarriage."

"Shit! How dreadful. I'm sorry you had to go through that."

"It is what it is. Most men disrespect women. You only have to watch the daily *News at Ten* to realise how prevalent it is these days. I'm sworn off men now, have been for years. I tried to sit Tina down and point her in the right direction, but she refused to listen. The key to her relationship with this fella was the amount of dosh he flung her way. He was slightly older, too. Maybe she was crying out for a father figure in her life. Was I to blame for that?"

"I doubt it. Please don't punish yourself thinking along those lines."

"I know it's going to linger, to cripple my logical thinking over the coming days."

Charlie entered the room, putting an end to the maudlin conversation. Katy smiled, appreciating her partner's kind gesture.

They sat there quietly as Mrs Lascombe sipped at her tea while staring at a spot on the wall ahead of her. Eventually, she heaved out a sigh. "Thank you, that was just what I needed. Hot and sweet for the shock. Shouldn't you be going now? What are you doing towards the investigation?"

"Our main priority in the first few days is to gather as much evidence from the scene as we can and to let the next of kin know of any fatalities."

"Now you've done that, what's next?"

"Now the real work begins. If you're sure you'll be okay, we'll be on our way."

"I'll be fine. I'll get to the hospital soon. I'm sure the news will hit me later. Maybe having the appointment so near is what's holding back the grief."

"Possibly. I'll leave you a card. If you think of anything we might not have covered and feel it's important to the investigation, don't hesitate to get in touch."

"I will." She showed them to the door and gently closed it behind them.

"Crap, that was tough. Thanks for offering to make the drink, I think it helped." Katy set off towards the car.

"Not sure I would be that composed if someone told me my only daughter had died."

"As I said back there, people deal with grief in different ways. Let's hope neither one of us have to deal with something like that in the future." Her thoughts lay with her daughter and the health scare she'd suffered a few years back which had terrified the shit out of AJ and her.

"I suppose. Where to now?"

"Back to the station. Let's see what the team can tell us about the main victim and confirm it's Tina's body, even though we're pretty sure it is."

*T*he incident room was as quiet as a library when they arrived. "All right ladies and gents?"

They all looked up from their screens and nodded. Karen motioned for Katy to join her.

"What have you got, Karen?"

"Plenty in the archives about Ray Thatcham."

"Such as?"

"He's seen as a do-gooder in the community. Has raised several million for a dozen or more charities."

"I'm surprised to hear that. What type of charities?"

"Mostly helping to raise awareness for the youth in our society."

"Raise awareness to what?" Katy asked, perplexed.

"Anything and everything."

"How strange. Okay, I'm more than a little shocked to hear this. I put him down as a player, not someone willing to give back to the community."

"Maybe it's a smokescreen," Charlie suggested.

"To stop the likes of the police digging into his business dealings, is that what you mean?"

Charlie shrugged. "Maybe. There again, I could be making it up as I go along because I can't think of another viable explanation."

Katy smiled. "A plus for not stating the obvious and being willing to think outside the box. Keep digging, Karen. Any news on what type of business he's running? I know he's an exporter, but do we know what that entails?"

"I'm still checking."

Katy turned to face the rest of the team. "Anyone got anything else? No, wait, we've got something I should mention. According to a sergeant with Thames Valley Police, there were four people on the boat when the police boarded. What we need to find out is who the other two people were and what they were doing there."

Graham was the next member of the team to speak up. "I might have some news on that front, boss."

Katy walked towards him. "Go on, Graham."

"I chased up the house-to-house enquiries not long ago and discovered a man reported seeing two men in sopping wet suits running along the footpath. They jumped in a black Range Rover which seemed to be waiting for them."

Katy nodded. "That's something. Could he describe these blokes? Is it worth him sitting down with a police sketch artist?"

"I can follow up on it, if that's what you want."

"Yes, do it, Graham. Did the witness say if they came from the direction of the boat or not?"

"I can check."

"Also, see if the boat was alight at the time or not."

"Will do." Graham reached for the phone and dialled a number.

Katy left him to it, stopped off at the vending machine to buy a coffee for Charlie and herself, and then went through to her office.

Graham rapped on the door a few minutes later. "Take a seat. Anything else for me?"

Graham sat and leaned forward in his chair. "Yep, Mike Wade told me he saw the two men running from the direction of the boat. He thinks he saw them get off it, but he can't be a hundred percent sure. When I pressed him about it further, he admitted that the men jumped off the boat before it hit the bank."

"Interesting. Did he say why he didn't mention that at the time?"

"He was too scared. He's since spoken to a family member who had urged him to do the right thing."

"I'm glad someone has made him see sense. What about the reg of the car, I don't suppose he gave you a clue there, did he?"

"Sadly, he said the car didn't have any plates, either front or rear."

Katy picked up a pen and threw it at the wall. "Bugger, that's not going to help us. What about any likely CCTV in the area?"

"Steve is looking into that now. He's called a few pubs along that stretch of the water to see if they can help us. Nothing as yet, though a few of them have said they have CCTV, but not at the rear of the property, only overseeing the car parks and the entrances."

"Not very helpful, but I suppose it makes sense. Okay, we need to find out more about Thatcham's associates in that case. I've ordered a warrant for his business address. I think what I'll do is order one for his home address as well. Something isn't sitting right with me on this one. Damn, I've also got the name of the other victim. Do me a favour and put Tina Lascombe's name on the whiteboard. We've just come from visiting her mother. Apparently, her daughter was having an affair with Thatcham."

"Did the wife know?"

"She knows now because we told her there was a female on board at the time of her husband's death."

"Are you thinking she might be behind this? A hitman situation?"

Katy raised her upturned hands. "Your guess is as good as mine. Hence the need for the warrant."

"Want me to check her bank accounts?"

"Yes, why not? Check into his as well, if you would."

"I'll leave you to your boring paperwork then." Graham exited the room.

Needing a break to give her whirring mind a rest, Katy called home.

"Hi, I was just thinking about you," AJ said cheerily. Georgina was in the background, nattering away to her dollies by the sound of things.

She smiled. "You were? What's going on there?"

"Munchkin is having a tea party for her dolls. I made cupcakes—correction, *we* made cupcakes—earlier to keep her amused, and now she's shoving them down the dolls' necks, whether they want to eat them or not."

"Hilarious. I don't envy you clearing up that mess later."

"Yeah, funny how that part slipped my mind when I came up with the idea. How's your day going?"

Katy rubbed at her temple with her free hand. "So-so, you know how it is at the start of an investigation."

"If you need to talk about things, I'm here for you, you know that."

"Of course I do. It's fine, baffling but fine. What else have you got planned today?"

He fell quiet for a few moments and then cleared his throat. "Nothing much, although, something big is running through my mind that I think we need to discuss later, if you're not too tired to listen."

"I've always got time for you. Sounds ominous, are you going to give me a hint?"

"Nope, not until I've slotted a few more pieces together in my mind. Then I was going to pluck up the courage to ring Mum, make arrangements to pay them a visit over the weekend. Do you think you'll be free?"

"Crap, there's no telling how this case is going to pan out. I'd hate for you to make the arrangements and have to back out at the last minute. Oh, what the heck! Go on, do it. It'll be better if we get things out in the open soon, rather than keep delaying the inevitable. I hope they don't cause trouble."

"Hey, stop it. I won't allow them to. Anyway, we're as solid as granite. No one and nothing anyone is likely to say or do is going to change that either. If they kick up a fuss, we'll leave. I've got all the family I'm ever going to need. Except...no, we'll discuss it later. You're busy now."

"Christ, talk about leaving me on tenterhooks. Can you give me a hint?"

"Nope, that would give the game away."

"Bloody tease. I'll make you pay. I have ways, you know."

"Hmm...if you're referring to bedroom antics...bring it on, baby."

"You can never keep a good man down, as my mother always used to say during my teenage years."

AJ laughed. "Are we still talking about a bedroom situation here?"

"AJ! Wash your mouth out, talking like that in front of our one and only child."

"Okay, about that…it's okay, I'm joking, I promise. I can just imagine your mouth hanging open in shock."

"You're not wrong there. Right, now you've raised that subject again, for the millionth time, I'd better crack on with my job. Love you, see you later. Hugs and kisses to Georgie."

"Mummy sends kisses, Georgina. What do you say, sweetie?"

"Bye, bye, Mummy! Love you."

Tears of joy welled up. "What I wouldn't give to be with you guys full-time, living on a remote island somewhere."

"You'd get bored within no time at all."

"I would not. We'll talk later. Enjoy the rest of your day. See you around six-thirty, if nothing important crops up in the meantime."

"Just ring me if it does."

She ended the call and got stuck into her paperwork.

*S*everal hours passed before she broke the back of it and left the office. She did the rounds with the team. Steve had secured some interesting CCTV footage from one of the pubs which showed the men getting on board the boat.

"Interesting. They seem like unwelcome visitors to me. Are you getting the same vibe?"

Steve nodded. "Yep. I had to switch cameras as the picture was too grainy on this one. Wait a second while I change discs."

"Okay, you do that and let me know when you're ready." She moved on to see what Karen had to say about the family's finances.

"Anything, Karen?"

"Define anything?" She chortled. "Bloody hell, this woman can shop for England. I mean, who in their right mind spends a hundred grand in one outing at a boutique?"

"Someone with too much money to their name, I should imagine. Apart from shopping expeditions, are there any other large payments we should be concerned about?"

"She must have bought a new BMW from the garage for over eighty grand."

"Bloody hell, how the other half live, eh?" Katy shuddered at the thought of spending that much on a piece of metal that gets someone from point A to point B on a map.

"Sickening, isn't it? Apart from that, I can't see anything that strikes me as odd. I'll keep digging, go back six months or so, shall I? If I can stand it," she added, disgruntled.

"Yep, if you would. Great work so far as it kind of puts her in the clear, if there are no large sums paid out to a possible hitman, for now. It's always good when we can say that."

Katy drifted back to Steve's desk. "Have you got the next one lined up yet?"

"I have."

"Interesting. Let's run it through, frame by frame and see what we can ascertain from it."

"The two goons in suits boarded the boat here. Looks like one of them had a gun, which matches up with the police report. According to the river police, the reason their guys boarded the boat was because a member of the public reported shots being fired."

"Bugger. Okay, can we see where and how the gun was used?" Katy peered closer at the grainy image. "Why is it we never get a decent image from these bloody cameras? Wait, was that a spark?"

"Yep, the goon fired his gun." Steve zoomed in closer.

Katy pointed. "The girl, is that her on the deck?"

"It is. Bloody hell, they tried to keep control over him by hurting her."

"Bloody figures. Sodding cowards. Personal views aside. One of the goons is now manhandling her, taking her downstairs."

"Makes sense, she'd be less of a distraction then."

"Wait. There's a scuffle broken out. Another gunshot?"

"Looks like it. Ray's gone down as if he's been hit."

Katy nodded. "Patti took a bullet out of his side. Shit, who are these men? Can we run their faces through the system or is it too much to hope for, that we get a hit from these shoddy images? It should be compulsory for these places to have decent cameras installed."

"I agree. Okay, the police boat is coming alongside. Ray ties the rope over the rail there to anchor them. Two officers climb on board. There's a discussion, and then the officer reaches for his Taser. Another two shots from the gun. Fuck, both officers go down."

Katy closed her eyes for an instant and said a silent prayer for the two brave officers. "What the actual? One's not moving. Bugger, the other one appears to be pleading for his life, that's what it seems like to me."

Two more shots lit up the screen. "They refused to listen to him and shot him at point blank."

Katy shook her head. "Killed in the line of duty with just a bloody Taser gun at their disposal."

"It's nonsensical and beyond me," Steve replied.

"Ray seems irate. It would appear he's struggling, possibly asking to seek medical help for himself and the girl."

"He asked but he didn't receive any. The boat starts up. The goons untied the police boat to set it free."

"I'm going to need to source another disc. Hold on a sec, boss."

Katy smiled. The adrenaline pumping through her system made her throat dry up. She bought the team a coffee, and by the time she and Charlie had distributed the cups, Steve had the next instalment ready to view.

"The boat's travelling at excessive speed, not sure I'll be able to keep up with the action for long," Steve said. "This is the final source of footage from the pubs along that stretch of the river."

"It is what it is, Steve, nothing we can do about it."

They watched the boat speed down the river, being chased by a second police cruiser and round the next bend. That's when the footage ended.

"Okay, at least it's given us an insight into what went down. A useful account for when we haul these guys in for questioning."

"Will the footage stand up in court?" Charlie asked then took a sip from her coffee.

"In my opinion, it'll be hard to discount. Who knows what the CPS will say, though, or the defence for that matter? Let's cross that bridge when we come to it."

4

---

*I*n a warehouse in the East End, Robert Anderton paced the floor, seething. "I told you to get the frigging boat off him. I wasn't bothered about the drugs. I needed that boat, and now it's gone up in bloody smoke. I'm holding you fuckers responsible for screwing up my plans. That boat would have come in handy over the coming month for what I have in mind. But no, you two knobheads had to do things your way."

"We're sorry, boss. We got flustered when the cops showed up."

"They're bound to show up if you fire a fucking weapon in the heart of London. Jesus, have your brains packed up and gone on holiday or something?"

"Yeah, I mean, no, boss," Caves replied.

Anderton threw him a warning glance which forced him to shut his trap. "Now, when people screw my plans up there's only one punishment I can think of. You're aware of how I work and what you got yourselves into. Which one of you is going to volunteer to pay the penalty?"

Stitch and Caves glanced at one another, their eyes wide with fear. Each of them pointed at the other and said in unison, "Him."

"What the fuck? You guys are really starting to tick me off now.

Grow some balls and pick one between you. Go over there and discuss it and then come back here and tell me what you've decided."

Stitch and Caves ambled across to the other side of the room and, amidst the pile of high-stacked crates, they held a conversation which ebbed and flowed between calm and irate tones.

"Well? I'm waiting," Anderton bellowed.

The men returned, and each of them shrugged.

"And what the hell is that supposed to mean?"

"Er, we can't decide, boss," Caves mumbled in his deep voice.

Anderton glanced over at the other two men in the room, Monty and Rex, one blond and one bald but of equal stature. "Who do you think should be punished?"

"It ain't up to us, boss," Monty replied, the first to chicken out.

Anderton threw his arms up in the air and slapped them against his thighs. "Fucking hopeless. Maybe I should get shot of the lot of you. I need men I can trust around me. It's clear none of you fit the fucking bill any more. Why is that? The money not good enough for you? I pay the going rate for knuckleheads with brains the size of petit pois." He laughed. "You don't even fucking know what I'm on about, do you, Caves?"

The man scratched the side of his face and ran the hand up past his caved-in temple, the feature which was attributed to his nickname, and through his short, cropped hair. "Never heard of it, boss."

"And there we have it. Okay, based on that answer alone, you're the one. Get him prepared," he demanded.

The other three men hesitated but only for an instant. Caves tried to make a run for it but the other three heavies pounced and tackled him to the floor. A fight ensued, three men the size of champion heavy-weight boxers against one of similar stature, fighting for his life.

Eventually, the three men managed to pin Caves to the floor. Stitch sat across his legs and the other two guys pinned each of his arms under their knees.

"Get the fuck off me. I ain't done nothing. Boss, I'm sorry, if you think I screwed up. Let me make it up to you."

"I don't *think* you've screwed up, mate, I *know* it. Now, name your instrument of torture." Anderton crossed to the other side of the room and wheeled a stainless-steel trolley, laden with hand saws, pliers and knives, and parked it close to where the men were.

"I don't want to die. I've just got engaged to the missus."

"Shut your fucking mouth. Every time you speak, you piss me off more. I think we'll go with the saws this time."

Caves screamed and wriggled, trying his best to shake off the men suffocating his movements.

Anderton picked up his implement of choice and leaned over Caves. "This is going to be a slow job, I ain't that handy with DIY tools. Just warning you so you know what to expect." He let out a wild laugh.

Caves shouted, calling his boss all the names he could think of as he made the first cut to the top of his right arm. It took nearly a minute for Anderton to chomp through the man's flesh, muscle and tendons. Sweat broke out on Caves' forehead and ran into his hair at the sides. He screamed. "Shit, don't do this. You're killing me."

"That's the idea, you motherfuckin' useless shit."

"Boss, that'll do, surely. Let him live, he's a good guy really," Stitch finally found his voice to speak out for the man who had been his constant companion on numerous jobs for the last five years.

"Honour amongst evil bastards, who'd have thunk it? You're telling me you want to swap places with him now?"

Stitch shook his head. "I didn't say that."

"Then keep your frigging mouth shut."

He bowed his head in shame. Caves looked at him, a look that told him he was grateful for attempting to intervene.

Anderton completed his task and held the man's arm up in the air. "One down, one to go. Hang tight, moron."

"Don't do it!" Caves screeched.

The other three men all took it in turns to stare at each other, as if questioning their boss' motives, but none of them dared to voice their opinions.

Anderton changed his choice of implement to a long-bladed

kitchen knife and returned to lean over Caves to remove his second arm. This time Caves hollered and passed out.

"Damn, he's gone and spoilt all my fun now. Never mind, on with the show, we have work to do this afternoon."

He then struggled to get through the muscle and tendons in the man's legs but eventually managed it. At the end of his strenuous ordeal, he felt the man's neck, looking for a pulse. There wasn't one; hardly surprising, considering the amount of blood that had squirted and drained from Caves' body in the last thirty minutes.

Anderton stood and glanced down at his bloodstained light-blue suit. "Well, this fucking whistle and flute won't see the light of day again…neither will he." He laughed.

The three men rose to their feet and stared down at what was left of their colleague.

"Right, let this be a lesson to you going forward, men. Either you carry out my instructions to the letter or suffer the consequences. None of you are indispensable, you got that?"

The men nodded their agreement.

"Get out of my sight and return here in an hour, no later. I need to go home and get changed. We reconvene here at three on the dot. A second later, and you'll get the same punishment. I have deadlines to keep, and any fucker who slips up will end up going through the same treatment, you hear me?"

"Yes, boss," Stitch replied.

"Don't be sad, Stitch. You'll have a new recruit soon enough. I've got another bloke joining us this afternoon. Now get out of my sight."

He marched out of the warehouse and into his waiting car. The driver scrambled out of his seat and opened the back door for him, his mouth gaping open at the state of his clothes.

"I had a bit of an accident."

"Oh my, do we need to get you to a hospital, sir?"

Anderton chuckled. "Nope, just take me home to get changed."

"Yes, sir. Right away." The driver closed the door and stared at the warehouse entrance until Anderton tapped on the window to get his attention.

"Now, as in, I'm in a bloody hurry."

"Yes, sir." The driver ran around the front of the car and dived behind the steering wheel.

Anderton leaned back against the headrest and breathed out a sigh, jubilation his prime emotion, not an ounce of remorse. He was thrilled with his achievements for the day, and it was only half over.

That'll keep the men in line, fuck them!

*T*he gang reconvened an hour later. Anderton was content to see the three remaining members of his intimate team all gathered at the warehouse ahead of the allotted time.

"Right, let's move on from what happened earlier, shall we? We have work to do and people to rob." He laughed and glared at the men standing before him who neglected to join in. He could sense a long, hard battle ahead of him. They'd get over the loss of Caves soon. If they didn't, well, that was up to them. He had plenty more torture techniques up his sleeve which he was willing to try out.

His driver interrupted his flow a few minutes later. He entered the room accompanied by a blond man-mountain.

"Gentlemen, say hello to your new colleague. Good of you to join us. Maybe you should introduce yourself."

"Thanks. I go by the name of Ken. My true name is Kentrovski, but most people have problems remembering it. I am Russian and I came to UK three years ago."

"Stitch, he'll be your partner."

Stitch nodded and fist-pumped the newcomer who moved positions to stand alongside him.

"Now we're back to full strength, here's what I expect from you."

Anderton ran through the plans and, once the men had accepted their responsibilities in the task that lay ahead of them, he sent them on their way, instructing them to return within a few hours with their haul.

5

The call came in at around four-thirty that afternoon. Katy had been winding the day down in her office when Charlie barged into the room.

"What's wrong?"

"Eye witnesses say a gang of men in suits jumped a bloke outside his pub, beat the shit out of him and stole his Porsche 993 Speedster."

Katy held up a hand. "Wait, is that supposed to mean something to me? A car is just a car, isn't it?"

"Not if you're a collector. This is a truly expensive one, apparently, not that I know anything about them. I looked it up, and it's as rare as a red diamond."

"Is there such a thing? I thought diamonds were...okay, we're going off track here. So the owner is still alive?"

"At the moment. He has life-threatening injuries and is on his way to hospital."

"Poor bloke. What does this have to do with our team, Charlie?"

"I might be way off the bloody mark here, but something clicked with me. Men in suits... What if there's a connection to the case we're investigating?"

Katy stood, grabbed her jacket off the back of the chair and followed Charlie out of the office. "Okay, you've convinced me. My brain was in a mid-afternoon lull there for a second. Let's get over to the scene. Where did it take place?"

"I'll fill you in en route." Charlie rushed out of the door.

Katy motioned with her head at the rest of the team. "I wonder how long her eagerness is going to last. More to the point, I hope her eagerness doesn't exhaust me in the meantime. We'll be back soon. Do the usual in our absence, folks. Find out who the victim is, his next of kin, just in case he doesn't make it. Also, see if there've been any other problems in his recent past for us to go on. See you later."

She raced down the stairs and found Charlie leaning against her car bonnet fiddling with her mobile.

"Now's not the time to be playing with that thing," she chastised.

"Ugh, you should know that's not me by now. I was researching the car and how many of those particular vehicles have been made over the years, if you must know."

"Sorry, my mistake. Hop in, you can do that on the way." Katy drove out of the car park. "Umm…it might be an idea to tell me in which direction I should be heading."

"Sorry, I got distracted. I have the postcode, I'll put it in the satnav. I'm not really with it."

"Everything all right, Charlie?" Katy asked, concerned.

"Fine. Just trying to do my best to impress my new boss and in danger of screwing everything up in the process."

"Nonsense and pack it in. You're doing well. There's no need to try and impress. Actually, you'll impress me more if you just be yourself and work methodically, the way you always have. I know you're a decent copper, Charlie, so let's make a concerted effort to improve that but in a natural way. Ugh…am I making any sense because it sounds to me like I'm talking a lot of gibberish?"

"I have that effect on people. Okay, here's where we're going, and I'll try to rein in my enthusiasm, how's that?"

"Sounds good to me."

The pub they were after was around a fifteen-minute drive away. The cordon had been set up, and SOCO were in attendance.

"Good, James is here. He'll give us the lowdown without any misguided shit." Katy waved at the lead technician who walked towards them.

"Hello again, ladies. We must stop meeting like this, otherwise people will start spreading rumours about us."

"That wouldn't surprise me. Okay, give us the details, James."

"The man, an Ethan Johnson, owns this establishment." He leaned in closer. "Well-to-do place, not your spit-and-sawdust type of pub, if you get my drift."

"Meaning what?"

He shrugged and smirked. "A mere observation which might help your investigation, dear Inspector."

"Thanks, I'll bear it in mind. How badly hurt was he?"

"He was barely alive when the ambulance got here. They managed to stabilise his breathing. Their fear is that he's suffered internal bleeding. You should chase that up with the hospital."

"I intend to. Any actual witnesses around for us to speak to?"

He pointed at a group of women huddled together in the far corner of the car park.

"What? Couldn't you have told them to wait inside?"

"Not very gallant of me, was it? Sorry. I knew you wouldn't be long. That's my excuse and I'm sticking to it."

"Never mind. I'll get to them in a moment. What about the car?"

"What about it?"

"It was stolen, why?" Katy asked, surveying the scene.

"Who the hell knows? A bit overkill to have four blokes rob the car, don't you think?"

"Four of them? Shit, yeah, that doesn't sound right to me. Any CCTV cameras around...? Ah yes, I've spotted a small one. Okay, if you've got nothing else for me, then Charlie and I should get on."

"Nope, nothing else."

Katy pulled Charlie away and leaned in. "Round up the women. Let's get them inside out of this cold wind. I'll go on ahead and have a word with the bar staff, see what they can tell me, if anything. Hopefully they'll have some footage from the cameras to show me."

"I'll do that. See you inside."

They separated, and Katy trotted into the pub's main entrance. The bar staff, all five of them, stood behind the huge mahogany bar which was shaped like the bow of a boat.

She showed her ID. "Who's in charge here?"

A woman in her thirties stepped forward. "I suppose that would be me. I'm Belle. Is Ethan going to be all right?"

Katy smiled and shook her head. "The honest answer is, I don't know. He's in the best place possible for him. Can you tell me what happened here?"

"Yes, I think so. This is usually our quiet period. Ethan asked the staff to attend a meeting. We have an important function taking place on Saturday in the marquee out the back…shit, should I ring and postpone that? Oh God, what a mess. I don't know what to do for the best. What if Ethan doesn't make it?"

Another woman reached out and stroked Belle's arm.

She turned and smiled at her. "I'll be all right, I think. It's just hit me, what lies ahead of us."

"Ethan will be okay, love. We'll cope, we can do this with your guidance."

"So much pressure."

Katy's heart went out to the woman. "I'm sure you'll cope if push comes to shove. You appear to have a good team of people by your side."

"I have. Thank you. Anyway, Ethan was in here. We were about to start the meeting. There were a few punters drifting in and out, so he got on with the meeting, and we took it in turns to serve the customers in between. He suddenly realised he'd left some important paperwork in his car and went outside to fetch it. We never thought anything more about it until some women came in screaming. They told us they'd seen a man being attacked outside. We all rushed out to find Ethan…lying where his car is usually parked. That was his baby. I guess he put up a fight to prevent whoever it was from stealing it." She shook her head and wiped away a tear with the sleeve of her jumper.

Katy rubbed her arm. "Try not to get upset, think positively. I'm sure he'll pull through."

Belle's chin wobbled, and she looked at the people coming in through the front door accompanied by Charlie. "I don't think so. His breathing sounded horrible. My sister's a nurse. I know that doesn't make me an expert, but it sounded to me like he had a punctured lung."

"The hospital will do their very best for him. Try not to worry. I'm sure he'd want you to ensure this place continued to run properly. I have to ask if you have any CCTV footage I can view."

Belle turned to speak to a younger member of the staff. "Taylor, you know a bit about the cameras, could you help the officer on that front?"

"I'll do my best."

"That's brilliant," Katy said. "Can I come round?"

"Go to the end, and Taylor will point the way. I hope you find what you're looking for."

Taylor showed Katy through to an impressive office with trophies lining a bookshelf along one wall.

"What are they for?" Katy peered at the inscriptions.

"Ethan is always on the go, whether it's running a marathon for charity or rock climbing and the like. I think there's one or two there for hang-gliding. That appears to be his favourite off-the-wall ultimate sport at present."

"Do you get on well with him?" Katy picked up the note of affection in his voice.

"Everyone does. He's a likeable character and he always treats his staff well. I love working here, it's so much better than the last pub I worked at. Ethan is so laid-back, not an ogre like some bosses can be."

"That's good to hear. I'm sure he'll be okay."

Taylor shook his head, and his mouth turned down at the sides. "I didn't want to say anything in front of the others because they're trying to keep positive, but it didn't look good to me. I saw the expression on the paramedic's face. He noticed that I'd spotted it and gave me a smile, but his eyes told a different story, I can tell you. You get an inkling about these things, don't you?"

"Sometimes. Hey, try not to think about it. If Ethan is a fit guy, then there's every possibility he will surprise you all and pull through this."

"I hope you're right. Let's try and find you what you need. I should've thought about doing this before you came, sorry to disappoint you."

"Don't be so hard on yourself."

Taylor worked swiftly and efficiently, and within minutes he had the disc playing what had happened on the twenty-one-inch TV screen. Katy watched a black Range Rover pull into the car park. It sat there for at least ten to fifteen minutes.

Taylor pointed at the screen. "That's Ethan. He's heading straight for the car. I told him he should keep it stored somewhere safe. Not sure I'd drive around in something as rare as that. He told me he'd worked hard over the years to obtain such a beauty and had no intention of keeping her locked away and not using it on a daily basis, and now look what's happened…"

"I'm with you, I'm not sure I'd flaunt my success in the shape of a rare car either."

They both stared at the screen as the horrifying events unfolded. The men pounced on the distracted Ethan. He never knew what hit him by the look of things. Two men pummelled him into the ground, then they tried to kick the life out of him. Even when Ethan's body stopped moving, they continued to attack.

"Jesus, they're fucking animals…sorry for swearing, I don't usually, but damn, that was bloody excessive."

"You took the words out of my mouth," Katy replied. "No wonder he's fighting for his life. Tell me, do you recognise any of the men? I'm glad we've got a good angle on them, that's sure to help us ID them."

"No, never seen them before. Why do you think they did it? Just to take the car, is that it?"

"I have no idea. We'll need to try and find out who these men are in order to obtain the answers. Would it be possible for you to give me a copy of the disc?"

"I'm sure I can figure out how to do it, if you can give me five or ten minutes."

"I'll leave you to it. Thanks, Taylor, I appreciate your help, I know that must have been uncomfortable for you to sit through."

"Hey, at least I wasn't on the end of that drubbing. I hope Ethan recovers from it."

"We're all hoping the same." Katy issued a taut smile and left the office to return to the bar. "Belle, another word if I may?"

The young woman approached Katy again. "Of course. Did you get what you need?"

"I did, it was very insightful. I wondered if you could give me a bit of background on Ethan. If you can't, would anyone else here know?"

"I think I'm the closest to him." Her cheeks coloured up a little.

"Sorry, are you two an item?"

She lowered her voice. "Not really. We have a kind of relationship. Oh God, that sounds awful. He bent my ear when he was drunk after hours one night, and one thing led to another and…you know what I mean."

"I do. Sorry if this has affected you more than the others. I take it he didn't have a significant other in his life then?"

"Yes, he has a steady girlfriend, Hattie. But his wife died in an accident a couple of years ago. Rocked his world, it did. I don't think he's ever got over her. He was distracted…gosh, you know, when we were having sex." She winced at the admission.

"I understand. What about his family? Does he originate from around here?"

"Yes, he's a London boy through and through. His father is still alive, but his mother died when he was ten. Heck, I should've called him as soon as the paramedics took him to hospital. What the hell is wrong with me?"

"It's fine. I can do that if you have his details."

"They'll be in the office somewhere. Give me a second."

She left the bar and returned with a sheet of paper with a number written on it. "Are you sure you don't want me to do it? It might be a shock for him if the police ring up."

"How about we do it together? He's not in ill-health, is he?"

"No, I don't think so. If he is, Ethan has never mentioned it."

Katy called the number, and an elderly man answered the phone. "Hello, sir. Would you be Ethan Johnson's father?"

"I am. Who is this?"

"This is DI Katy Foster of the Met Police, sir. I'm at your son's pub now and I'm calling to inform you there's been an incident."

"What type of incident? Is Ethan all right?"

"No, sir. He's on his way to hospital."

"Damn. Which hospital? Give me the name, and I'll go there immediately. What's happened to him?"

"I'm sorry, I'll need to check which hospital has taken him. I think it'll be St Thomas' but I'll have to get back to you on that."

"Do it. I demand to know."

He slammed the phone down. Katy felt a fool for not having the information to hand. "I'll be right back. I should've checked." She raced around the bar and out through the main entrance.

"Is something wrong?" Charlie called after her.

"No, it's fine. Carry on." Outside, she scanned the area and spotted James close to the scene and, keeping her distance because of her lack of protective clothing, she shouted, "James, I need to ask you something."

He glanced up. "Go on."

"Did the paramedics say which hospital they were taking Ethan to?"

He pulled a face. "Sorry, they didn't, and I didn't think to ask."

"Shit. Okay, that makes two of us. I'll get on the phone."

"Try St Thomas', that would be my first port of call."

"Yep, I'll do that. Thanks." She took a few steps back and pulled up Google on her phone to search for the number. She dialled it and tapped her foot while she waited for the automated system to work through its options and then pressed four for the Accident and Emergency department.

A friendly female voice came on the line. "Accident and Emergency, how may I help?"

"Hi, I'm DI Foster from the Met." She gave the woman her ID number. "I'm trying to trace a patient who was picked up from a pub car park in Newington. The patient's name is Ethan Johnson."

"Let me take a look on the system, hold the line."

Katy tapped her foot some more until the woman returned.

"Ah, yes. We have him here."

"Thanks, that's all I need to know. I'll be there shortly."

"You're welcome. See you soon."

Katy called Ethan's father back to confirm the details. "Hello, sir, it's DI Foster again."

"Well, get on with it. Where is he?"

"He's in the A&E at St Thomas'."

The man mumbled a thank you and hung up.

Katy stared at her phone. "You're bloody welcome."

She went back inside.

Charlie came towards her. "Everything all right?"

"Yes, how are things going with you?"

"I'm nearly done. They've all said pretty much the same thing when I've spoken to them individually."

"Good, no, that's excellent news and will strengthen our case against the men once we get our hands on them. Or should I say if?"

"No, don't think that way, boss. It's very early days yet."

"It might well be, but we could be dealing with five murders in the space of twenty-four hours with no damn clue as to the motivation."

"You're connecting the crimes then?"

"Aren't you? Men in suits—all right there were four this time instead of the two in the Thatcham incident—and a black Range Rover spotted at both scenes. Oh, I forgot to mention that we have pretty clear CCTV images this time. I'm hoping that will lead us to figuring out the identities of these men sooner than anticipated."

Charlie's face lit up, and she smiled. "That's brilliant. We should be celebrating that fact."

Katy shook her head. Experience told her otherwise. "Don't count your chickens just yet. It's all too easy. I get the impression these guys possibly want us to find them for some reason."

"You do? Why?"

"I haven't worked that part out as yet. I'll let you know when I figure it out. Right, let's finish up in here. You get back to the witnesses, and I'll question the staff again, see if they can add anything. Once we're done here, we'll need to shoot over to the hospital. I feel it's my duty to be there for when Ethan wakes up, if he ever does. I've notified the man's father, he's on his way over there now. Are you all right to tag along or is Brandon expecting you?"

"Don't worry about me, work comes first when we're involved in a murder case. Something I learnt from my mother."

"Of course. She wasn't around much while you were growing up, was she?"

"No. I don't hold it against her, it's the job. It gets under your skin, doesn't it?"

"As much as we try our best not to let it consume us, I don't know an officer who leaves a case they're running at work. It's tough on our other halves at times."

"I'm beginning to understand that. I hope Brandon does. I think he'll be a lot cooler than my dad ever was."

"Glad to hear it, he seems a good lad. Hark at me, old lady that I am." Katy chuckled and headed back to the group of staff who were standing in stunned silence.

"Belle, I've contacted the hospital and informed his father where to go." She lowered her voice to say the next part. "I know you said you had 'a thing' with Ethan, but can you give me the girlfriend's number?"

"Yes, hang on. Let me get my phone." She took two paces, retrieved her mobile from the shelf under the till and scrolled through it.

Katy extracted her phone from her pocket and poised her finger ready to input the number as she read it out.

Once she'd dialled, she moved to the end of the bar to conduct her call in private, away from flapping ears.

"Hello?"

"Sorry to disturb you, Hattie, you don't know me. This is concerning Ethan."

"Okay, who are you?" There was a note of caution in her voice.

"I'm DI Katy Foster. I'm truly sorry to have to inform you that Ethan has been involved in a crime."

"Wait…what sort of crime? You're not making any sense."

"Unfortunately, Ethan was assaulted in the pub car park. He's just been transferred to St Thomas' hospital."

"Oh heck! Is he badly hurt? Ignore me, he must be bad if he's in hospital. How badly hurt is he?"

"It's hard to say. We arrived after the paramedics had left. They're treating him at A&E now. Would it be possible for you to go to the hospital?"

"Of course. I'm babysitting a nephew at the moment, my sister is due back anytime. Bloody hell, I'm scared what I'll find when I get there."

"It would be better to go there prepared, I think. Are you up to driving?"

"I think so. Yes, I'll take a few deep breaths and get my act together. Thank you for ringing me."

"It's okay. I'll probably see you there shortly, after I've spoken to the staff here."

"Was anyone else injured? Was it an attempted burglary or something?"

"Everyone else is fine, and no, I don't think it was an attempted burglary, although saying that, Ethan's car was stolen in the attack."

"Jesus, that's his pride and joy. He'll be devastated to hear that. Why would anyone attack him just to rob a bloody car?"

"It's surprising what folks will do these days. I take it the car was insured against theft, yes?"

"Oh yes, he paid a hefty sum every year to cover it against all possibilities."

"Good to know. I don't suppose you know if there's some form of tracking device on it?"

"Maybe. I can't think off the top of my head."

"Never mind. We'll look into it."

"I'll try and have a think on the way. I'll go now, if that's okay?"

"Sure. See you soon." Katy ended the call and returned to the cluster of staff. "Any of you guys talk to Ethan about his car, specifically, what type of security it had on board?"

A young ginger-haired lad raised his hand slightly. "We were always discussing it, and yes, he had a GPS tracker on it."

"Excellent. Has he had it long?"

"It was the first thing he added when he got the car," the lad confirmed.

"Thanks for that. Okay, my partner and I are going to leave now and head over to the hospital. Will you guys be all right here? Will you keep the pub open?"

"It's what Ethan would want," Belle replied as she tucked a lock of stray hair behind her ear.

"I'll leave a card. If anyone thinks of anything that I should know about regarding the incident, please call me immediately, day or night."

"We will, won't we guys?" Belle asked.

The rest of the group either nodded or said yes.

"You will do your best to get these men, won't you?" Belle asked, fear evident in her bright-blue eyes.

"You have my word. Let's hope your boss pulls through this. Stay positive in the meantime."

"We will."

"I'll get a uniformed officer to drop by and take statements from you all during the day." Katy gave a brief wave and left the group to join Charlie who was in the process of winding things up with the witnesses.

They thanked everyone for their time and left the pub.

Katy marched across the car park to James. Keeping her distance, she called out, "We're going to shoot off now. I take it you haven't found any evidence yet?"

"Correct. What about the cameras, anything there?"

"Yep." Katy waved the disc in the air. "We'll be going over it in the morning."

"I hope it produces something useful. See you soon, no doubt."

"Pretty much guaranteed living in this neck of the woods, James."

. . .

*A*round fifteen minutes later, Katy and Charlie raced through the main doors of the hospital and followed the signs for A&E.

Katy flashed her ID at the receptionist. "I called earlier about an Ethan Johnson."

"Ah yes, I remember. There's been no news so far. His father has arrived and is waiting in the family room."

"Thanks, we'll go and see him. Any idea how long before we hear any news?"

"Sorry, there's no telling with cases like this. I can request the doctor to come and see you when he has a spare five minutes."

"That would be wonderful. Thanks for your help. The family room is where?"

"Bottom of the corridor on the right. You might want to take a coffee with you. The only vending machine on this level is over there."

"Thanks for the tip." Katy bought two drinks and rejoined Charlie.

They walked into the family room to find a man in his early sixties, pacing the room, a pained expression on his tanned and weathered face.

"Hello, sir. Are you Mr Johnson?"

"I am and you are?"

"We spoke on the phone earlier. DI Katy Foster, and this is my partner, DC Charlie Simpkins."

"Ah, I see. Maybe you can use your powers of persuasion to get some information out of the doctors around here. They've dumped me in here and told me someone will be along soon. I just want to know what's going on with my son, is that too much to ask at a time like this?"

"It's not unreasonable, sir. I checked with the receptionist on the way in. She's passing on a message for a doctor to see us when he has the time. Until then, I'm afraid we're going to have to be patient."

"That is not something I'm known for, having patience. Do you know what happened?"

"We've come here from the pub. It would appear four men attacked your son. It seems stealing his car would have probably been their motivation."

"I knew it! I told him to be careful buying a bloody car that expensive, but would he listen to me? No. Now look what's happened to him. I just want to know what's going on, this is all rather frustrating for me."

"Can I get you a drink, Mr Johnson?"

"No, I don't want a blasted drink. All I want is information."

"It'll come in time. They're obviously busy in there, working on making sure your son is comfortable. I'll give the doctor another ten minutes and then chase him up."

"Ten minutes is going to seem like ten weeks to me." He kicked out at a chair leg, sending it scuttling into the one beside it.

Katy turned her back on him and rolled her eyes at Charlie. *Just what we need. While I agree with him feeling frustrated, showing his anxiety isn't going to help matters.*

She sat on one of the orange plastic chairs and sipped at her drink. Charlie did the same, leaving a few seats between them.

There was a strained atmosphere shadowing the room.

The door opened a few minutes later, and a blonde woman in her twenties walked in. She glanced at Katy and Charlie and then ran into the arms of Mr Johnson. "Oh, Des, isn't it awful? Have you heard anything yet?"

He smoothed a hand over her mane of golden hair and then took a step back to look into her face. "Thanks for coming, Hattie. No news yet. The detective over here assured me she'll chase the doctor up soon."

Katy smiled at the woman. "I was the one who rang you. Thanks for coming."

"I couldn't not come. He's my world. Oh, Des, what if he...?"

"Hush now. Let's not even contemplate that, love."

Hattie sniffled. "But it's there, in my mind, I can't shut it out."

"You're going to have to, for now."

The door opened a second time, and everyone in the room held their breath as a doctor came in and closed the door behind him.

"Hello, are you the Johnson family?"

Katy jumped to her feet and offered an explanation as to who everyone was. "Mr Johnson's father and girlfriend, and we're the two detectives dealing with the case, Doctor."

"I just wanted to bring you up to date on what we've ascertained so far about Ethan's injuries."

"Is it bad?" his father demanded.

"I want to lay my cards on the table and tell you that, as things stand, your son's condition is classed as critical. I'm sorry if that's not what you were expecting to hear but I think it's important not to give people false hopes at this stage. We're doing our utmost to alter that situation and to offer you more hope. At present, we're losing the battle. That's not to say we've given up on him yet, however, with the injuries Ethan sustained in his prolonged attack, well, his body is fighting hard to overcome many obstacles on the road to improving his situation."

"That's all well and good, Doctor, but what does all that mean?" Mr Johnson asked.

"It means that with one perilous injury, your son's life would be in immense danger. He has several, which is causing us to scratch our heads."

"What sort of injuries are we talking about?" Katy jumped in to ask, her heart rate rising rapidly out of fear for the victim.

"I don't want to be away from him for too long. Briefly, he has three broken ribs, a punctured lung and possible damage to one of his kidneys. We're in the process of arranging an emergency MRI scan which will give us the answers as to how damaged the organs are and if we're dealing with any internal bleeding. My guess is that's very likely. I have to get back now. Hopefully, I'll be able to answer any questions you may have fairly soon."

"Thank you, Doctor. Don't let us keep you," Mr Johnson said. He draped an arm around Hattie's shoulder, and with her head resting on his chest, she broke down.

Katy followed the doctor out of the room and trotted beside him back to triage. "No bullshit, Doc, what are we looking at here?"

"Honestly, the prognosis isn't good. He's barely clinging to life. I have to get back to him. Please, do not tell the family this, but I don't think he's going to make it."

"Damn. Please do your best for him."

"I will, I assure you. I'm not in the habit of losing a patient, no matter how devastating the injuries. I'll keep you all informed."

"Thank you." Katy tried to peer through the door the doctor sped through in his haste to get back to his patient. A young man lay flat out on the bed, attached to several monitors with a couple of nurses checking his wounds and his vital signs. Her heart sank. She slowly made her way back to the family room.

Three sets of eyes glanced her way as she entered.

"I did my best. He couldn't tell me anything more." She hated lying, but it was only a white lie in her eyes. One that would protect the family from the terrible truth. They were stuck in a waiting game now.

Katy returned to her seat, and Charlie gave her a reassuring nod. At least her partner appeared to appreciate the turmoil she was going through.

The wait was excruciating and went on another thirty minutes or so until the young doctor reappeared. "Hello again. I'm sorry, we did all we could to try and save Ethan, but he slipped away from us a few minutes ago. His injuries were just too severe for his body to handle."

Hattie screamed, and Des Johnson cradled her in his arms as the colour drained from his cheeks.

Charlie reached for Katy's hand and squeezed it. Katy shook her head, and tears of frustration dripped onto her cheeks which she swiftly wiped away.

"Thank you, Doctor. For all you've done," Katy said, finally finding her voice.

"I wish the news could be different. I'm sorry for your loss."

Des just stared at him, a lost soul on a deserted island of grief.

The doctor left the room again.

"Is there anything we can do?" Katy asked, not really knowing what else to say to the grieving couple.

Des pointed over Hattie's shoulder at Katy. "You can get out there and find the bastards who did this. I'm warning you now, if you don't find them, I'll make it my life's ambition to track the fuckers down and kill them one by one."

"While I appreciate how angry you are, sir, that kind of talk is not going to help the issue. I'll give you my assurance that my team and I will do our very best to bring the culprits to justice. Please, we don't want any type of vigilantism going on."

"Then get out there and find them. I know what you lot are like. Why do you think there are so many cold cases in the bowels of the police stations in London, eh? I listen to the news. Well, now this affects me and my family, and I promise you, mess up, and I'll make sure I take things higher, and I'll have no hesitation in getting the press involved either, you hear me?"

Hattie ran a hand down his arm.

"Yes, loud and clear, Mr Johnson. Some officers might see your words as a threat, but not me. I can see you feel passionately about your son's death and are in the throes of grieving for him. We'll be in touch with you as soon as we have any news for you."

"And don't forget to look back on what happened to his wife while you're at it. It was no accident, I guarantee you."

"We'll be sure to do that, Mr Johnson."

Katy and Charlie left the room.

"When did Ethan's wife die?" Charlie asked.

"Two years ago. Seems a bit bizarre he should mention it, expecting us to delve into it, but then again, he might have a point. Who bloody knows?"

6

K aty ordered the team to go home at around eight that evening. Her joints ached through weariness and tension during the drive home. A sadness rifled through her that she had missed Georgina's bath time that evening. She had made a promise to herself to always be there for that. She realised now how unrealistic that assurance had been. Her job would need to interfere at times. She hoped it wouldn't happen too often.

Women coppers have it tough, trying to balance work and their home lives at the same time!

She smiled, appreciating how lucky she was to have a more understanding husband than most women in her position. Being an ex-copper, he was aware of what she was up against on a daily basis.

She couldn't wish for a better partner, or husband as he was now. She had a feeling that was going to take some getting used to, calling AJ her hubby. She couldn't be happier, though. Life had dealt her some major blows in the past, but her recent trip to the registry office had to have been the highlight of her life to date. She just hoped her parents saw it that way when they eventually told them.

We'll deal with that another time.

She entered the house and tugged off her shoes, shocked to see her ankles were swollen. Although she shouldn't really be surprised, after the day she'd had. She crept into the kitchen. AJ was at the stove, stirring the contents of a frying pan. She slid her arms around his waist and rested her head on his back. Closing her eyes, she inhaled the scent of his aftershave. She'd missed him.

He swivelled to face her. "Tough day?" He kissed the tip of her nose.

She raised her head and smiled. "Better now I'm home with you. How was Georgina at bedtime?"

"She missed her mummy, but we got over that hurdle."

"You're so good with her. I wish I could be a better mother to her, that's my biggest regret taking on this role."

"Don't think that way. You're an exceptional copper, you deserve to be an inspector not a sergeant. It'll take you some time to settle into your new role. How's your new partner doing?"

"I think she's going to be an asset to the team, the signs are good so far. Something smells nice, what are we having?"

"I thought you deserved a treat so splurged on a nice piece of fillet."

"You shouldn't have, but it's most welcome. Have I got time to get changed and pop my head in on Georgie?"

"Go for it, I can delay things for ten minutes."

"Great. Thanks, love." She kissed him and, forgetting how tired she was moments earlier, sprinted up the stairs. Creeping into the nursery, lit by a carousel night light, she crept towards the small lilac princess bed. Her heart filled with a mixture of joy and disappointment. *Will it ever get any easier?* She knelt down beside the bed and swept back the stray hairs covering Georgie's rosy-cheeked face. Her eyes fluttered open. *Damn, I've woken her.* "Go to sleep, baby."

"Mummy, is that you?" Her eyes closed again.

Katy smiled. "It is, darling. See you tomorrow." It was a struggle to leave Georgie's bedside, and she would have willingly curled up in a ball on the floor and gone to sleep if her stomach wasn't grumbling angrily. She jumped up and crept out of the room again and made her way into the bedroom. After having a quick wash, she changed into her leisure suit and returned to the kitchen to find AJ had a glass of red wine waiting for her.

"I thought you could do with one of these."

"You're a mind reader. Hey, you, what was that phone call about earlier? You have an idea you want to run past me."

"No, it can wait, you're exhausted."

"I've always got time for you. Go on, hit me with it."

"After dinner, okay? And no, that's not me skirting around the issue. The dinner needs to be served up now or it's going to be spoilt."

"My tummy is agreeing with you, so you win this bout."

A few minutes later, AJ placed a delicious meal in front of her which consisted of steak in a peppercorn sauce, grilled tomato, corn on the cob, mushrooms and chips. "Bloody hell, I'll never be able to eat all this."

"Do your best, what you can't eat I'll have to force myself to finish."

"How come you never put on weight, even though you're always chucking food down your neck?"

"Great genes, I suppose." He grinned and savoured his first mouthful of steak. "Eat up, you have cupcakes for afters."

Katy sniggered. "I can't wait. This is scrummy. Thank you for taking care of me so well."

He roared. "Idiot, you don't have to thank me, we're a partnership. You do all the hard graft, and I get to spend time with our adorable daughter, making cakes and having a blast every day. What's not to love?"

"Don't, I can feel my envy gene twitching. Come on, tell me what you were hinting at earlier."

He placed his knife and fork down and picked up his glass of wine, delaying his response. Katy had a feeling what he was about to say was going to turn their world upside down.

"God, the trepidation is killing me," she whispered.

"Okay, it's nothing big, not really. What am I saying? It's huge, that's what it is…"

"AJ, will you spit it out? Oh my God, you're not pregnant, are you?"

"I think that would be taking the role reversal situation a tad too far, don't you?"

"Yes, possibly. I'd have a dozen kids if it was achievable, however." She grinned and scooped up a forkful of buttered mushrooms.

"Right, well, I don't know how to tell you this really."

"Just say it. Oh God, joking aside, you're not going to tell me you're leaving me, are you?"

His mouth gaped open for a second. "Now you're seriously being ridiculous. Do you not think I would've done that before we got married at the weekend?"

"Married people have more rights." Her rebuttal came before she had a chance to engage her brain. The hurt expression told her she'd said too much. She covered his hand with hers. "I was joking."

"Some things shouldn't be said in jest. I can't tell you how much I love our life."

"I know, I feel the same way. Forget I said it. Now stop teasing me and tell me."

"Okay. I was sitting here the other day, thinking about what I could do to bring in some extra cash while Georgie is at nursery. You know I'm not one for sitting around doing nothing all day."

"All right, and what have you come up with?"

"A kids' entertainment package."

"A what?"

"Starting up a business to entertain the kids at parties."

Katy thought over the idea and chewed on her bottom lip. "What would that entail exactly?"

"Hiring clowns, jugglers, people who make animals out of balloons, that sort of thing."

"It sounds expensive to me. How much will it cost to set up, love?"

He waved a hand. "I need to work out the intricacies of it yet, but I'm sure I can make a go of it."

"You know you'll have my backing for whatever you decide to do in the future, but we haven't really got the funds, not right now. Any form of business will involve setting-up costs. You'll need to buy equipment for a start, how much will that be?"

"That's just it, I won't. I'll hire the experts in. All I'll be doing is acting as an intermediary, if you like."

"Oh, I see. Like an agent to the acts? Or have I got that wrong?"

"Yes, similar. What do you think? It shouldn't cost much, should it?"

"I don't know. I think it's still going to cost around ten grand to set you up. We're short of readies, love, you know that."

His gaze dropped to his wine glass that he was twisting in place. "Umm…there's a solution to that."

Katy inhaled and prepared herself to be shocked all over again. "Go on. What do you mean?"

Avoiding eye contact, he said, "I could ask my parents for the money."

Katy dropped her knife and fork on her plate and pushed it away. "But we promised we would never go cap in hand to them after the way they treated you."

"I know we did, but I can't think of another option, can you?"

"You haven't given me enough time to consider anything. Let's sit on this for a few days. Mull the idea over and make a list of pros and cons. If we can't find a solution, then you'll have my blessing to ask your folks. Do you think they would stump up the cash? Bearing in mind we've yet to tell them about the wedding. We're expecting them to kick off big time about that."

"Yeah, maybe that part slipped my mind. Okay, let's ignore that particular conundrum for a moment. Do you think the actual concept is a good one?"

"In theory, yes. If your parents don't volunteer the funds, how likely is it that a bank will lend you money?"

AJ sighed and twisted his mouth. "I never thought of that. Maybe I should delay it a few months then, is that what you're saying?"

"No, not at all. Just don't jump in feet first. Cover all the bases, and we'll go from there. If you go to the bank, they'll expect you to have some form of business plan to present to them. Have you worked that out yet?"

"No, nothing so far. Maybe we can sit down when you have a spare moment, and you're not too tired, and create one?"

"Of course. Want to tackle it this evening?"

"No way, you're dead on your feet. It can wait a few days. I'll draft a couple of ideas tomorrow during the little one's nap."

"Good. You're determined enough to make anything work, AJ. I'm so impressed you are trying to make our lives better."

"Thanks, it's nice to hear. Now, have you finished?"

"I have, it was delicious. Not sure I could manage a cupcake, though. Maybe I'll pass on pudding tonight."

"Are you sure? Georgie made a special one, just for you."

"Maybe I should eat it when she's present in that case."

He cleared the table and filled the dishwasher while Katy topped up their glasses with the remainder of the bottle. He appeared beside her with a plate holding a huge cupcake with 'Best Mummy' written in blue icing on the top.

"Oh my, how precious is that? Was it your idea?"

"Nope, she wanted to do something special to show how much she loves you."

"Oh shit, don't start me off. You're doing a remarkable job with her."

AJ shook his head. "Correction, *we* are. It's a partnership, one that I envisage going from strength to strength in the future."

"I'm lucky to have you. Let's discuss your business ideas this evening, I'll be fine, I promise. The sooner we get the ideas fixed in place the sooner you can get the ball rolling. I'm so proud of you."

They shared a kiss which backed up her sentiment.

"Ditto. Go through to the lounge. I'll grab some paper and pens from Georgina's stash."

. . .

he following morning on the drive into work, Katy's head was churning with AJ's plans. Initially, she'd had her doubts if a children's entertainment business could work, but the more she thought about it, the more she realised what a fantastic venture it could be for AJ. The only downside would be the costs involved in setting up such a business. If he made the right contacts from the outset, it really needn't cost him much. She prayed AJ had enough restraint not to ask his parents for the money, although she would completely understand him going down that avenue if all the options he tried weren't fruitful.

She was distracted, still wrapped up in her thoughts, when she parked the car outside the station.

"Oh, hi, Charlie. How are you?"

"I was beginning to wonder if I'd done something wrong."

Katy frowned. "Sorry, is that supposed to mean something?"

"You drove past me, staring right at me. I waved, and you ignored me."

"You did? Bugger, sorry. Honestly, I didn't even see you."

"Is something wrong? Is Georgina okay?"

Katy waved the suggestion away and pushed through the main entrance. "No, nothing like that. I'll tell you about it later, if we get the chance. It's nothing to worry about."

"Okay, it's up to you. A problem shared and all that…"

"I know. It's not a problem as such." She turned and smiled at the desk sergeant. "Morning, Mick, anything we should be made aware of at this hour of the morning?"

"Morning, ma'am. I don't know how to tell you this…"

A sense of foreboding descended. "Shit! Why don't I like the sound of that?"

He shrugged. "Sorry. Around five minutes ago, I received a call to say a gentleman had been killed outside his home in Tooting."

"Okay, is there more to the story than that? I'm guessing there is."

"Yep. He was about to get in his Ferrari when four men pounced, beat the crap out of him and drove off."

"With his Ferrari, I take it," Katy replied, her stomach clenching and tying itself into knots.

"Correct. I was about to ring you but figured you'd walk through the door within minutes, so I left it."

"Have you got the address for us?"

He held out a sheet of paper. Charlie took it as she was closest to the reception desk.

"Do me a favour, Mick, let the rest of my team know about this and ask them to do the necessary, ie, put a trace on the vehicle and source any likely camera footage in the area. Bloody hell, four men, what the fuck is going on? Excuse my language," she said, quickly checking the area in case any members of the public were sitting there. The room was clear. "Come on, Charlie, let's get going. There's no telling how long it'll jeffing take us to get out there at this time of the morning. Needs must, though."

"Leave it with me," Mick shouted after them.

They raced across the car park and joined the crush of traffic heading into the city. They'd need to turn off soon, so hopefully things would speed up for them then.

"What do you think's going on?" Charlie asked. Her leg had developed a nervous twitch and was juddering.

"Well, if it's linked to the other cases we're working on, there has to be a connection to the cars…saying that, as far as we know, Ray Thatcham didn't have his car stolen, did he?"

"Nothing has been reported along those lines so far. What about his boat? Do you have any idea how much they cost? That one used to be a beauty before the fire took hold. Maybe the men were trying to rob it when the river police showed up."

Katy assessed what Charlie had come up with and nodded. "If that's true then I'm impressed you should think of that. However, being cautious, I have to ask why the thugs didn't succeed in taking the boat and were seen running from it. Would they leave a high-value treasure like that to burn?"

"Maybe our lot showing up like that was enough to scare them off."

"Perhaps. I suppose we'll find out soon, hopefully. Let's try and think why someone would be stealing expensive cars."

"To sell to the highest bidder?"

"Maybe. Here's what I don't understand: why send four heavies in to steal the cars and kill the owners in the process? Where's the sense in that?"

"Money. People will go to extremes where money is concerned. Do you think we should get the team looking into it? Or is it too early to suggest that?"

"No, I agree. Let's face it, we've got no other possible leads to work with at present. Make the call, get Karen to do the search for us. She's more likely to come up trumps than the others, but those words never left my lips, okay?"

Charlie snorted and placed the call. She hung up a few minutes later. "She's on it. Do you think the pathologist will be at the scene?"

"I should've asked Mick. I just presumed she would be. Do you want to check for me? Here, use my phone, it's under *Patti*. Give her a call on my behalf." Katy passed her mobile over to Charlie.

Her partner made the call and then handed back the phone. "She's running late. I hope I didn't upset her, she was a little brusque with me."

"Don't worry about it. She can be a tad tetchy at times. Her focus is usually on the crime scene."

"Thanks for the warning. I'll try and not to take things to heart in the future."

"I'm delighted with what you've achieved so far, Charlie. I have no reservations whatsoever about you being my partner, so do me a favour and relax. Not too much, just enough to enjoy yourself. What am I saying? You get what I mean, right? You're not stupid."

"I understand. What you're telling me to do is take a chill pill but don't get so chilled that I end up horizontal."

"Perfect. Why couldn't I find the words to say it like that?"

They both laughed. Katy indicated and left the mounting traffic behind. She knew a shortcut to the area they were heading, so there was no need to use the satnav on this occasion.

Katy drew up at the edge of the cordon. The body of the victim had been covered by a white sheet and was in the actual curve of the cul-de-sac. "Let's hope we have a few witnesses we can count on."

"You'd think so, given the location."

Charlie and Katy stepped out of the vehicle and went to the back of the car to retrieve two sets of protective clothing. They flashed their IDs at the uniformed officer on guard, and he held the tape up for them. Off to the left were two SOCO vans.

"Let's see what Patti has to say about this," Katy said.

A couple of the technicians were in the process of erecting a marquee to protect the corpse from the threatening grey sky.

"Hi, Patti, we meet again," Katy said, her tone more cheerful than she felt.

"We do. As you're here, does this mean you think there's a link to the other cases you're dealing with?"

"Stands to reason, doesn't it? How many times do you get called out to a murder scene where the victim's car has been stolen?"

"Point taken. We'll wait until the tent's up and then dive in."

"I don't suppose you've had any results back yet for the other victims?"

"Not yet. The first ones are due back later this afternoon. I'm doing my best to rush things through for you, Katy."

"Thanks. I don't have to tell you how much I appreciate that."

"It wouldn't hurt to say it now and again." Patti smirked.

"Get you. I'll be sure to remember that in the future."

"I was kidding. Let's just say you're one of the more likeable inspectors I have the pleasure of working with."

"High praise, coming from you. I'll take it. Have you assessed the vic's injuries?"

"I have. You haven't noticed anything, have you?" Patti wiggled her eyebrows.

"Such as?"

Patti stared at the victim's covered body and then pointed at something just beyond the sheet.

"Good Lord, is that a leg?"

"It is. Don't go reaching for the sick bucket, it's a prosthetic one."

"His?"

"Of course, unless he hopped around on one leg and someone else jogged by and mislaid their artificial one."

"All right, there's no need to be sarcastic."

Charlie laughed. "Have you listened to yourselves? You two are so funny."

"Believe me, it wasn't my intention to add a dose of humour to the crime scene," Katy replied. "Getting back to the man's missing limb, do you think the perp tried to torture him and possibly got more than they bargained for?"

Patti hitched up a shoulder. "Who knows? Poor bloke."

"Do we know who called it in?" Katy glanced around at the bystanders hovering by their gates, a few alone and some choosing to be with other neighbours in a cluster.

"I haven't got a Scooby. Maybe uniform will know. Almost there with the tent."

"I'll be right back." Katy walked towards a uniformed officer who was speaking with a member of the public, a wee elderly lady whose face lacked any colour. "Can I have a brief word, Constable?"

"Yes, ma'am. Excuse me, Mrs Drake, I'll be right back."

"Take your time, it's not like I'm going anywhere soon with your lot blocking the road."

Katy smiled and took a few paces to the side. "Is she the one who called it in?"

"She is. Spiky sort. Softly-softly approach with her."

"You're doing a fabulous job. Apart from complaining about being restricted, has she given you anything of use?"

"She said she opened her curtains at about seven-thirty this morning and noticed the victim, an Otis something, she can't remember his surname."

"It doesn't matter, we can sort that out later. Go on."

"She noticed him come out of his house, even waved to him. He waved back—friendly sort, apparently. Then she went into the kitchen to see to her pussy, her words not mine, and put the kettle on. She sat and ate her breakfast for the next ten to fifteen minutes, added a few items to her shopping list. We're delaying her getting to the supermarket before ten, her usual time."

Katy rolled her eyes. "The joy of getting older and getting stuck in a routine." She sighed. "And?"

"And then she went upstairs to hop in the shower. She pulled the curtains in the bedroom at around eight-thirty, and that's when she saw him lying in the road. She rushed out to see if he was all right—she used to work in a care home. Anyway, she felt for a pulse but couldn't find one. She called the ambulance and the police."

"Damn, so she did see the culprit or plural then?"

"No. However, I asked around, and a young man said he saw four guys get out of a black…" He looked down at his notebook.

"Range Rover?" Katy filled in for him.

"Yes, I believe that's correct. The chap was in a rush, said he's got a tyrant of a boss and had to leave for work. I've arranged to return at five-thirty to take down his statement."

"Good. Did he give you an inkling into what they looked like, or perhaps tell you the car reg?"

"No. There was no stopping him. I tried to delay him; he was having none of it, though."

"Bugger. Not very helpful then."

"Sorry, I did my best."

Katy patted his forearm. "I'm frustrated, not with you, just the situation. These guys will be long gone now. If only people would understand how difficult our job can be at times."

"Agreed. Maybe he'll come up with something significant later when I return."

"We can live in hope. The old dear can't tell us anything else?" she asked, sensing she was clutching at straws.

"Not really."

"Okay, I'll leave you to it. At least we have a rough idea what happened. Can you make sure you ask all the neighbours for me and get down their statements if they saw anything to do with the crime?"

"I'll do that. Spend all day here if I have to."

"Thanks. I'll be sure to remember you at Christmas."

"I'll hold you to that, ma'am."

Katy left the constable and darted back across the road.

Patti and Charlie were discussing personal stuff, centred around Lorne.

"Sorry to interrupt."

"You're not," Patti replied. "Anything of use from that mob?"

"Yes and no. The old dear was the one who called it in. She saw Otis"—Katy pointed at the horizontal corpse—"coming out of his house. Waved to him and went about her day out the back. After she'd had her shower, she pulled the curtains and saw him on the ground and rang the police."

"Sod it! She didn't see the culprits then."

"No, but a young man did. He saw four men arrive in a black Range Rover, attack him and steal the vehicle."

"Okay, if that's the case, how come it was the old lady who made the nine-nine-nine call?" Charlie enquired.

"Pass. The constable told me he tried to prevent the man from leaving but he refused to hang around, gave the excuse that his boss is a tyrant."

"Oh really? Does that sound legit to you, Katy?" Patti shook her head in despair.

After mulling it over, Katy announced, "No, but it's all we've got to go on. I'm thinking I should chase the young man up at work, get the facts for myself and not delay."

"I'd be inclined to do the same," Patti replied.

"Did you get where he works?" Charlie asked.

"I didn't. Go and ask the constable if he took down the information. If he didn't, then we're screwed."

Charlie set off and returned a few moments later, shaking her head. "We're officially screwed."

"Ha…and I didn't feel a thing," Patti piped up.

Katy suppressed the smile threatening to erupt.

The technicians gave Patti the go-ahead to enter the tent. Katy and Charlie filed in after her.

Patti carefully uncovered the corpse and placed the sheet on the plastic square a few feet away. "What have we got here then?"

Katy glanced down and winced at the bruising on the man's face. Her gaze drifted down his body. "I can't see any open wounds, can you?"

"Nope. Let me check his head."

She ran a hand underneath his head, and when she checked her glove it was smeared with blood. "It would appear he took a whack to the head. That could have been enough to kill him. Maybe it was accidental. What if his leg came loose and he lost his footing and dropped to the ground, banging the back of his head during the contact?"

"Sounds plausible to me. You'll probably be able to back that claim up after you've cut him open, won't you?"

"I will. Let's get the photos taken. Give us five minutes, and then I'll assess the rest of his body, see what other wounds or contusions I can find."

Katy and Charlie left the tent again. A photographer passed by, opened the flap and entered.

"That poor man. Do you think him losing a leg shocked the goons?" Katy asked Charlie.

"Undoubtedly. It's not the type of thing you see every day, is it?"

"Can you ring the station? Try and get his surname from the electoral roll then see if a member of the team can find a next of kin for him."

Charlie found a quiet spot on the close to make the call while Katy surveyed the area. No cameras in sight, but she felt there was enough to go on to link the crimes. Although, the first crime scene was still puzzling her, and she couldn't put a finger on why. She sighed, the two latest victims' faces running through her mind as she contemplated the pain they'd had to endure before their deaths. Why put someone through that just to steal a damn car? Why did it take four men to carry out the deed?

There were more questions than answers at present—annoying, but a fact all the same.

Charlie rejoined her.

"Anything?" Katy asked.

"Otis Casey, he's twenty-nine. Apparently, he lost his leg last year in an accident at work, it got caught in machinery. He received a substantial pay-out from his firm."

"Bloody hell, hence the Ferrari, and look where that got him. Any partner or wife in the picture?"

"Yes, he's engaged to a Caroline Armstrong, she's a model. Karen googled him, it's surprising what you can find out over the Net these days."

"Tell me about it. Okay, we'll have another brief chat with Patti and then get back to the station. This case is already ticking me off. We need to get our thinking caps on and piece together the elements to see what we do next."

"I agree. What about the statements? Want me to organise those?"

"I think the constable has it in hand. Check with him first, see if he needs any more resources or whether he's willing to take on the task himself."

Charlie set off.

Katy entered the tent to find Patti examining the corpse more thoroughly. "What have you got?"

"Severe contusions to the body, back and front. If I had to call it, I'd say the man took a pounding from someone's fists, finished off by a good kicking. Wouldn't surprise me if steel-capped boots were worn by the perpetrators."

"With the intent to cause the maximum damage, no doubt."

"You've got it. Sickening, right?"

"No cuts, as in, from a knife or similar weapon?"

"Nope, not from my initial examination."

"So he was beaten to death. Seems hard to believe."

"Believe it, the proof is all here."

"I suppose if there were four of them, it wouldn't take much to finish him off if they all took a turn." Katy shuddered. "Just to steal a bloody car. Had they asked him for the keys and warned him what would happen if he didn't hand them over, I'm sure he would've relented and willingly given them to the thugs."

"I'm afraid we'll never know. Any suggestions where you think this is leading yet?" Patti asked.

"Not really, nothing concrete anyway. I'm inclined to think along the lines that possibly it's gang related. These things usually are, aren't they? Someone stealing cars to fence them on the black market, possibly." Katy shrugged. "It seems too obvious, but that's all I've got, for now."

"Sounds feasible. Tough people if they're intent on killing folks for their possessions."

"Yep, I keep thinking that over and over. Shitty world, eh?"

"Tell me about it. Right, I must get on. I need to get this young man back to the lab."

"Good luck, I'll pass on the PM, if that's okay?"

"Sure. You have better things to do, I should imagine."

"Yep, I need to get back and thrash some ideas out with the team, after I track down his next of kin. Charlie said his fiancée is a model."

"Ouch. Good luck telling her. Does she work around the London area or is she one of these jet-setter types?"

"Yet to discover. See you later. Don't forget to ring me with those results."

"I won't. As soon as they land on my desk, I'll give you a bell."

Katy smiled and left the tent. Once outside the cordon, she and Charlie slipped off their protective suits and placed them in the waiting black bag. "Back to base. We have a lot to discuss."

"What about the fiancée?" Charlie prompted.

"Bugger. I just said to Patti we need to track her down. How easily she slipped my mind. Ring the station for me. I'll start the drive back and veer off if I have to. If she's a model, she might be working on the other side of the globe for all we know."

"True."

They got in the car.

Charlie made the call and tapped Katy on the arm, gesturing for her to pull over not long after they'd got on the way. "She's working near the London Eye, so her agency just informed Karen."

"Okay, that shouldn't take us long to get there. Hang tight, I'm going to use the siren, it's an emergency after all. I'm fed up with getting stuck in traffic."

"I hear you."

*T*hey arrived at the London Eye which, according to the sign, was closed to the general public for the next few hours due to a photo shoot. An officious-looking man stood at the entrance to the tourist attraction. Katy and Charlie approached him and flashed their warrant cards.

"The police? We've got permission to be here, we're not doing anything wrong."

"We didn't say you were. We'd like a word with Caroline Armstrong, if that's possible?"

"I'll have to see. We're on a tight schedule, you see, they're only allowing us to take over this place for a few hours."

"I understand that, but it's urgent that we speak to her."

"Urgent you say, may I ask what it's about?"

"You can ask, but I'd rather tell Miss Armstrong that in person. If you wouldn't mind fetching her for me. Thanks."

The man hesitated for a few seconds and then heaved out a sigh. "Very well. Marcel isn't going to be happy about this."

"Is he the photographer?"

"Yes. I'll get her."

They waited for the man to return. The pods rotated slowly until the one holding four people and lots of camera equipment came to a halt in front of them. A man with frizzy blond hair came hurtling towards them.

"What's the meaning of this?" he demanded in a slight foreign accent. "We are extremely busy and have a very limited time to get these shots taken today. No, Caroline can't see you, not now. I won't allow it."

"Sir, if you'd just calm down for a moment. We wouldn't be here if it wasn't important."

He glanced back at the pod and motioned for a tall brunette to join them. "Here she is. You have five minutes, that's all."

The brunette eyed everyone with caution.

"This is Caroline. You can have five minutes, no longer," Marcel repeated and then marched off in a huff.

"Who are you?" Caroline asked. She wiped a few drops of sweat from her brow with a small hand towel.

Again, Katy and Charlie showed their IDs.

"We'd like to ask you some questions, Miss Armstrong," Katy said.

"About what? I haven't done anything wrong."

"All will become clear soon. What time did you get here today?"

"We started early, around eight. I left home at six-thirty, or around that time. Why?"

"Did you see anyone strange loitering in your close this morning?"

Caroline wiped the moisture from her top lip. "No, such as who?"

"Okay, it was probably too early anyway. I'm sorry to have to tell you that your fiancé, Otis, was found dead after you left the house."

Caroline staggered backwards.

A young cameraman who was within striking distance of her charged forward and steadied her. "All right, Caro?"

"No...she's just told me...he's...he's dead."

The man turned to look at Katy. "What? Who's dead?"

"And you are, sir?"

"Roger. I'm a good friend and colleague of Caroline's. I repeat, who's dead? Oh God, no..." He faced Caroline again and touched her cheek with his right hand. "Darling, it's not Otis, is it?"

Caroline nodded and rushed into his arms. "How? He can't be..."

Roger swivelled around so he was staring straight at Katy. "Answer her, she has a right to know, damn you. Look at the poor girl, she's beside herself. She needs answers."

"I'm sorry. We can't give you any answers right now. Our duty is to tell the next of kin as soon as we possibly can, before we begin our investigation. I have to ask, did Otis have any known enemies?"

"Wait...don't answer that, Caroline. What are you saying? That someone killed him?" Roger frowned and hugged Caroline.

"Yes. We can't go into detail, not until the post-mortem has been performed. But yes, it would appear that he was murdered outside your home between seven-thirty and eight."

"No, this can't be true. Why would anyone want to hurt Otis, after all he's been through? Why?" Caroline wailed. She buried her head in Roger's shoulder.

"He's a lovely man. I've met him a few times. After what he's had to put up with the last year, well, I find it inconceivable that someone would want to kill him."

"I'm sorry, are you talking about the accident with his leg?"

"Yes," Caroline replied. "We went through hell together. Most of my friends said they could never have coped if their partner had gone through something similar, but I love him. He's the only man who has ever treated me right. Years of searching for a soul mate, and now he's gone. What am I going to do without him, Roger?"

"Hush now, sweetie. You're surrounded by good people. We'll get you through this, I promise we will. What are you doing about the person who did this?" he demanded.

"Our best. We've taken witness statements from the neighbours."

"They saw what happened? I bet they didn't try and help him, did they?"

"No. In all fairness, I think it all happened too quickly for anyone to lend a hand."

"Bloody cowards. We're living in a world of selfish cowards. If I ever witnessed someone being attacked, I'd dive in there," Roger vented his anger.

"It's not always advisable, sir. Always better to call the police first."

"Yeah, and what good would that do? Your mob are always slow to react to calls. My sister's flat was broken into last month, took your lot three days to show up at her door, despite her ringing several times to see where you were."

"That's unfortunate. There are certain crimes which take priority, of course. Something like Otis' case would be such a crime."

Roger went to respond, but Caroline urged him not to. "I don't want to know what could have happened to have prevented his death, what's the point in that? He's gone, and I want to know why. Who did it? Are they likely to come after me?"

"I would have said that's unlikely. We have reason to believe their motivation was to steal your fiancé's car."

"No, not Chérie? He was devoted to that car. Bought her with his compensation pay-out from his injury. I urged him to get something for himself even though he wanted to put the money towards a down payment on a house. I told him I was happy renting for a while, and now my income is steadily increasing we would be able to get on the property ladder in a few years, we'd just need to be patient. And now this…"

"Chérie, is that what he named her? That was sweet, love." Roger swept back the hair from Caroline's face and smiled at her.

"Yeah, it was precious. She was precious to both of us. Why aren't you out there looking for her?"

"We have a team back at the station trying to find the car. They'll be using all the resources available to them, I can assure you. Can you give us a rough estimate of what the car cost?"

"Eighty grand or thereabouts."

Roger whistled. "Holy shitballs! That was a huge wedge of money, hon."

"It was. She was worth it. He deserved it after what he went through after the accident. I didn't begrudge him spending the money on himself."

"Has anyone possibly approached him about buying the car in the past?"

"No, if they had, he didn't tell me. He would have shown them the door anyway. There was no way he would have got rid of her."

"What about friends or neighbours, has anyone paid more than a passing interest in the car lately?"

"Been infatuated by it, you mean?"

"Along those lines, yes."

"No, not that I can think of. Otis was the type who allowed

strangers to have a ride in the car. He was super thrilled to own her. I didn't see that as a negative, maybe I should have."

"It would be a start if you could think of anything out of the ordinary which has happened concerning the car in the past month or so. Did someone invite Otis to have a race or something along those lines?"

"Oh no, he would never have treated her that way. He respected her and always drove her carefully."

"Thanks. Okay, I'm sorry to have broken the news to you like this at work, but I appreciate you taking the time out of your busy schedule to speak with us."

"When can I see him? You know, to say goodbye..."

"I understand. The pathologist will call you directly and make the arrangements. Again, we're sorry for your loss. Here's a card. Call me if you think of anything else or if someone strange contacts you regarding the car."

She gasped. "They wouldn't, would they?"

"I doubt it, but just in case."

"I'll call you immediately. Will I be safe, staying at the house, or should I move out?"

"Perhaps consider staying with a friend for a few days, until things on the close settle down."

"You can stay with me, honey," Roger offered.

"Thanks, Rog, you're a special friend."

"We'll be in touch soon."

Katy and Charlie left the couple and walked back to the car.

"Was it my imagination, or was he overprotective of her?" Charlie asked once they were out of earshot.

"They did seem a little close. I'm getting the impression he's besotted with her. All she could talk about was the car and Otis, so I'm not sure it's reciprocated on her part. Needless to say, I believe it's something for us to consider."

7

"How many times do I have to tell you? You worry too much. Yes, I'm aware of the deadline you've given me. We have most of the cars, only one more to collect, and that will be sorted today at the latest." Anderton knew how to pacify his contacts when the need arose. He also knew when to vent his anger on his men, especially if they let him down, like Caves had.

He hadn't regretted his decision to kill a member of his team, not now the newcomer had slotted into place and was excelling at his job. He felt in control of his future once more. It hadn't always been the case, but recently, he'd shown his worth. Starting up this new sideline had improved not only his well-being but his bank balance to boot.

Apart from the minor setback of not nicking Thatcham's boat, everything in his world was smelling of roses.

He reached for the phone and dialled a number he knew off the top of his head. "Hey, baby, are we all set for tomorrow evening? I have something special planned for you."

"Hi, I was just sitting at my desk, thinking about you. What's on the agenda?"

"It's a surprise. Want me to send a car for you?"

"No. I'll make my own way over after work, if that's all right. No, wait, will I need to dress up for this surprise?"

He laughed. "I was thinking the opposite. Dressing down, or should I say, wearing no clothes at all would be my choice."

"Cheeky. It had better be worth my while. I've had a tough week so far."

"I know you have. I'll make sure I pamper you, I promise."

"Sounds like heaven. Hey, I have to go, I'm needed elsewhere. Oh, go on, pick me up tomorrow then."

"Always busy. Not sure how you have the time for me."

"Fishing for compliments again?"

He smiled at the sexy tone permeating her voice, and his dick stood to attention.

"Until tomorrow." He hung up, leaned back in his chair and imagined what lay ahead of them. Tomorrow night would be *the* night.

A knock on the door brought him back to the here and now. "Come in."

Scar-face Stitch entered the room. "Boss, I thought you'd want to know we've got the heads-up on the final car. Want me to gather the men together?"

"Yeah, do that. I'll be out in a mo. You all right, Stitch? It had to be done, you know that, right?"

"He was a good worker, boss. They're hard to come by in this business. If you were going to punish him then you should have involved me, too. Both of us screwed up, not just him."

"I had my reasons. Don't make me regret my decision, right?"

"Sorry, I didn't mean to question your motives. I'll get back to work."

"Yeah, you do that. I'll be out soon."

Stitch exited the room and closed the door behind him. Anderton rose from his chair and went over to the window to admire the wondrous view he had of the city. Moving to this building had been the highlight of this year. It proved how successful he'd become since starting the new business. He'd found where he belonged, the joys of running a team willing to do his dirty work for him, which gave him all the rewards he'd been searching for over the years, and now he'd have the woman he'd been craving to share in his success.

He let his smile drop and joined his gang. Stitch was standing by the podium where Anderton conducted his meetings. He took up his position and ran through their instructions, making sure each member of the team knew their responsibilities and what the consequences would be should anything untoward go wrong with their final mission.

"Once the car has been obtained, you need to arrange to get it to the dock ASAP. The container ship is due to leave tomorrow. Any delays…well, there won't be, will there?"

"No, boss. You can count on us, right, lads?" Stitch asked the other men.

The gang all nodded and shouted, "Yes."

"Okay, if there are no problems, let's get on with it."

8

The team were all gathered around the whiteboard. Katy cleared her throat to speak and glanced at the door when a figure appeared.

"Don't let me stop you, carry on, Inspector." DCI Roberts sat in a spare chair at the back.

"Okay, let's see what we have here. Four victims. Ray Thatcham, killed aboard his boat, along with the woman who appears to have been his mistress, Tina Lascombe. Two of our colleagues also lost their lives in this incident. The footage we've managed to obtain points us in the direction of two well-dressed thugs who were seen running along the towpath after the boat crashed into the bank. Did they set the fire on the boat? Or was it due to the impact? I have my doubts about the latter."

"Do we know who the men are yet?" Roberts asked.

"Not yet. We're still processing their images through the system. Annoyingly, it's taking time to get a result, sir."

"Okay, that's unfortunate. Carry on."

"It is. We haven't been sitting around twiddling our thumbs in the meantime, as you'll see when I reveal the next two cases which have come our way in the past few days. The second case is that of Ethan

Johnson. He was injured outside the pub he owned. The footage shows four men this time. They laid into him and then stole his rare Porsche. He later died from his injuries in hospital. There was no way he could have survived the brutal beating he received. His injuries included a punctured lung, several broken bones and damage to one of his kidneys."

Katy's gaze drifted around the room and landed on Roberts, expecting him to add something. He didn't, so she continued.

"The third case we're investigating has to be the saddest in my eyes, although they're all bad. Otis Casey was only twenty-nine. When we arrived at the scene, we discovered his prosthetic leg lying next to him on the pavement. Apparently, he lost the limb in some form of accident at work involving machinery for which he received a substantial compensation pay-out. He used the money from that to buy a Ferrari which, according to his model girlfriend, was his pride and joy. Again, four men were reportedly seen outside Otis Casey's house. They stole the car after they beat the shit out of him."

"Wait, so two high-value cars have been stolen. What about the first victim? Why are you linking the three cases?" Roberts asked, puzzled.

"That's right. The victim's boat was brand-new and worth a pretty penny, but it wasn't stolen, just torched. That part is perplexing and doesn't really add up to me. We're linking all three crimes because of the suited men. All right, there were only two seen at the first crime and at the others it appears that four men attended each of the crimes. Again, we don't know the reasoning behind that just yet."

"What if the two goons from the original crime screwed up? What if it was their intention to steal the boat and things went wrong, as in, the river police turning up when they did? Maybe they panicked and that's why they ran off," Graham piped up.

Katy thought his assessment over for a second or two and nodded. "You could be on to something there, Graham, actually, Charlie raised the same point earlier. So, guys, you tell me what your digging has come up with."

Karen raised a hand. "Nothing too much in the Thatchams'

accounts, general ins and outs. Although some of the high spends Mrs Thatcham has under her belt could be seen as dubious, I wouldn't say they're out of the ordinary for someone with money."

"Okay. When we visited Thatcham's business partner, he was the one who highlighted that Thatcham was having an affair with one of the secretaries. The question is, how did his murderers know they'd be on his boat and not tucked up in a hotel room somewhere? And what's the connection?"

Roberts shifted in his chair, and Katy sensed he was about to make a pointless observation.

"Setting the first case aside for the time being, what about the other two cases and the missing cars? Tell me you've tried tracking the cars down through the ANPR system."

"We've tried. No such luck, which is mystifying us. These types of cars would ordinarily stick out like a bloody sore thumb. Not this time. It's as if they vanished into thin air."

Roberts narrowed his eyes and chewed his lip.

"What are you thinking, sir?"

"I remember an occasion, not long after I arrived, actually, it was a case involving your mother." He pointed at Charlie. "Bloody hell, what am I saying? It was the case *you* were unfortunate to be involved in."

"When I was abducted by The Unicorn," Charlie mumbled.

"Yes, sorry to bring it up, Charlie, it could be important, though."

She waved a hand, dismissing his apology.

"We were chasing the fucker, and the car we were following suddenly disappeared. Had us scratching our head at the time. Until we figured things out, I can't recall who sussed it, it was probably that smartarse mother of yours," he said, smiling at Charlie who blushed under his gaze. "Anyway, whoever it was, we worked out that the vehicle we were chasing was driven onto a waiting lorry. Have you thought about that?"

Katy shook her head. "No, that hadn't crossed my mind. I'll get the team on it right away, thanks for the insight."

"I've been known to have my uses now and again. So, what do you consider we're looking at? Someone stealing the cars to order?"

"That's the conclusion I've come to."

"In that case, my advice would be to get the other departments involved, Organised Crime, Vice even. Let's get these fuckers off the streets and quickly."

"That's our intention. We haven't had much luck with the information we've received so far, sir. Patrick, something that came to my attention yesterday was that Ethan Johnson's wife died in a suspected accident a couple of years ago. His father seems to think there was more to it than that. Delve into it for me, see what you can dig up. I also have some questions about Thatcham's wife. Stephen, do some research into her background. She was livid when we told her there was a female aboard the boat. I'm not sure if she knew he was having an affair or not. Let's just say her reaction to the news of her husband's death didn't sit well with me."

"I'll see what I can find out, boss," Stephen replied.

"That's it for now then, folks. I'm expecting the results from forensics to come back this afternoon. Until then, let's hit the computers. No, wait, Graham, can you try and find out how many black Range Rovers are listed in a thirty-mile radius?"

Graham nodded. "I will."

Katy stared in Roberts' direction. He motioned with a nod to her office. She headed that way, and he joined her and closed the door.

"How's Charlie fitted in?" he asked.

"Really well. No qualms from me. She coped with her first PM admirably. Have you got doubts about her?"

"Me? Not at all. I reckon she'll end up giving Lorne a run for her money."

Katy relaxed a little and laughed. "Yep, me, too. We're lucky to have her. My only concern is when we come up against a real baddie, how she's likely to react. You know, given what went on back in her teens."

"You missed the test I gave her out there, then?"

"You mentioned that fucker's name on purpose?"

"I did. She handled it better than I expected. Don't worry about her, she's made of strong stuff. Lorne might have thought she let Charlie down in the past, but the opposite is true in my opinion. Charlie is far stronger than people give her credit for. Let's face it, to come through the horrendous ordeal with The Unicorn and want to join the police... well, I'm not sure how many youngsters would rise to that challenge."

"You make a good point. I suppose it helps her being amongst friends. She knows the team from the various get-togethers Lorne has put on over the years."

"True enough." He became reflective. "Carmen, Sara and I have attended a few of them."

"Everything all right, Sean—sorry, sir?"

"Don't correct yourself, it's Sean when we're alone, you know that." He sighed heavily. "I received my decree absolute through the post this morning. I suppose the situation hadn't fully hit me until I saw it in black and white."

"Damn, I'm so sorry things didn't work out for you. It's hard when there's a child involved."

"I'll see Sara as much as I can until another bloke comes on the scene. Not sure how I'm going to feel about things if and when that happens. But life goes on, right? Speaking of which, have you told your parents about the wedding yet?"

She placed a hand over her chest. "Nope, I'm dreading it. Maybe having a secret ceremony wasn't the brightest idea AJ and I have ever had."

"Not an ideal way to begin your marriage if you ask me."

"I know. I think the reality of the situation is only just dawning on us. Hey ho, what's done is done, nowt we can do about things now."

"Good luck, I fear you're going to need it. I'd better make tracks. I've got the monthly meeting to attend with the Super."

"Returning your best wishes for that one."

He left the room, and Katy expelled the breath she'd been holding in, and her shoulders sagged, releasing the tension that always took hold in his presence. She hated the thought of being checked up on. She understood he had a job to do, but preferred to do things her own way. She knew where he was if she needed any guidance during an investigation.

Katy settled behind her desk and picked up the phone. She rang an old colleague of hers, from her time up in Manchester, for advice. "Hi, Les, it's Katy Foster. Do you have a spare five minutes for a chat?"

"Katy Foster, well, now then, this is a blast from the past. How are you diddling down there in the smoke?"

"Not so bad. How are things with you? Still enjoying rounding up the scum of Manchester, are you?"

"Yeah, same old at this end. I hear you got promoted *again*."

"For my sins. This one was kind of forced upon me. It's growing on me, though. I also got married at the weekend."

He whistled. "Now that's a sentence I never thought I'd hear you utter. He's a very lucky man. I take it we're talking about AJ? That is his name, isn't it?"

"That's right. A natural progression for both of us. Georgina is nearly five now. He's been bugging me to marry him for years; I finally succumbed."

"A man with a lot of common sense obviously."

"I'll pass that on to him." She laughed. "Getting back to why I've called. I know you're Vice but I have a dilemma I need to run past you, if you're up for the challenge at this time of the morning."

"Hit me with it. You know I've always got time for you, love."

"Right, I'll give you a brief round-up of what I'm up against and I'd like your opinion, if that's all right?"

"Go for it."

She gave him the lowdown on the investigation so far and asked, "What do you think? Should I be looking at the underground crime scene?"

"Sounds like it. We've had a spate of similar offences going on over the years up here. They're either linked to gangs or possibly drug related. Either way, they haven't turned out well. Hang on, yes, we've had similar, however, what we haven't had is where they've killed the owners after robbing their cars. That's a double whammy. Totally uncalled for."

"Yeah, I agree. That's the part that was bugging me and why I sought your opinion. I'm scratching my head over this one."

"Rightly so. I'd be doing the same in your shoes. Do you have any idea who the culprits are yet?"

"No, we've got some pretty good visuals on them, but the system is being super slow, which hasn't helped our cause."

"Yeah, our guys have said the same this week. It's old and needs updating. Want to send me some pics? You never know, they might have moved area and could possibly be from up here. Stranger things have happened."

"I'll do that when I get off the phone. Take a gander and let me know. Thanks for your help, matey."

"Always welcome. Stay safe down there."

"Right backatcha."

Katy sorted out the images and looked up Les' number in her contacts. She sent him the files and waited for his response. Thankfully, it was almost instantaneous.

Sorry, I can't help you. Decent shots, though. Have you thought about asking the public for help?

Thought about it but dodged the idea. You know how I hate being in front of the camera.

Tell me about it. It might be your only option. Ring me if you need me.

I will. Thanks, Les. X

Ignoring the post piled on her desk, she returned to the incident room. "Anyone got anything for me?"

Karen looked up and raised her hand. "I have something interesting you might want to see."

Katy raced across the room and stood by Karen's desk. "I'm all ears. What have you got?"

"When I checked the Thatchams' bank accounts the other day, I put an alert up for any major transactions to come through. I've just received a notification that Ray Thatcham made two payments to two separate accounts around the time of his death."

"Very interesting. Do we know to whom?"

"Yes, two women. The first is an Alison Temple, and the second is a Katrina Banks."

"What sum are we talking about, Karen?"

"A hundred grand each."

"Wow, that's a lot of wonga. Let's see if we can trace these women and see what their connection is with the deceased."

"I'll get on it now and give you a shout if I stumble across anything."

"You do that. Anyone for coffee?"

The team all shouted back either yes or no. There was only one no, and that was Charlie.

Katy stopped by her desk. "Everything all right? It's not like you to turn down a shot of caffeine."

"I'm fine. I've decided to up my intake of water during the day, that's all."

"Go you. I know we should all do it, but I prefer coffee to the taste of nothing." Katy laughed. "Can you give me a hand?"

Charlie left her desk and followed Katy to the vending machine. "I hope the boss was kind to you once you disappeared into your office."

"He was. He asked how you were getting on. I raised a few concerns."

"What? You did? Why didn't you say something to me first? If you have a problem with either me or the way I work you should've told me first."

"Climb down off your high horse. I was winding you up. Actually,

I told him the reverse, said that you had impressed me beyond words since you'd started."

Charlie's cheeks turned crimson. "Aww…you didn't?"

"I did. I only speak the truth, Charlie. Now, if we can put our heads together and crack this case quickly, Roberts might have another dream team on his hands."

"That would be cool. It's a tough one, though. However, I did think the chief had a good idea."

"A possible truck hiding the vehicles once they've been stolen? Yep, I agree."

"I've been looking into it, checking the CCTV cameras around the areas, but haven't come up with anything yet."

"That's a pity, it could take hours to find a clue. Will you keep at it?"

"Of course. I'm not one to give up easily, you should know that."

Katy smiled. "I do. Hand these out, will you?"

Charlie distributed the drinks to the team and then returned to her desk.

"I'll be dredging through the post. You have my permission to interrupt my boredom at any time." She carried her coffee into the office.

Halfway through the mundane chore, she glanced up when Karen stuck her head into the room. "By the smile on your face, I take it you have good news for me."

"I have."

"Come in, take a seat." Katy placed the letter and her pen on the desk and put her hands together.

"I've managed to locate the two women through the electoral roll and then I searched Facebook to see if they had accounts on there."

"Good thinking. Tell me you hit the jackpot."

"I did. Both women are friends with each other. Looks like they have expensive lifestyles, and yet neither of them works, not from what I can tell."

"Interesting, don't tell me they're sex workers? Or possible escorts?"

"They might well be, except I've stumbled across something even better than that. Do you want to join me at my desk and I'll show you what I'm talking about?"

Katy tore out of the room after Karen.

"What the hell?" Katy said as she peered at the screen.

9

"Right, let's get these women in for questioning," Katy replied, excited and dumbfounded by the information Karen had managed to gather from the social media profiles for both women.

"Can I ask on what grounds?" Charlie said.

"Association to a wanted criminal. See for yourself. The evidence is as clear as day. These women are connected to the two thugs who were on board the boat the day Thatcham and Lascombe died."

"Whoa! And he transferred the money to their accounts before he died?"

"It seems that way. We need to find out why. Graham and Stephen, I want you to take two uniformed officers with you and collect them. Tread carefully. The first sign of trouble, I want you to contact the station and ask for backup, okay?"

The two men jumped to their feet, collected the women's addresses from Karen and raced out of the room.

After the two members of her team left, Katy went back to her office and called Patti to gee her up with the results.

"You read my mind. I was just about to ring you. I've got one report I need to reread. Give me five minutes to do that. I'll call you back soon."

Katy was left staring at the phone after Patti had hung up. "Great, that told me then. Hurry up, Patti. I sense things are going to come together quickly and I need to be prepared."

Charlie appeared in the doorway, her brow wrinkled into a frown. "Were you just talking to yourself?"

Katy bared her teeth in an awkward smile. "You might have overheard something like that. What's up?"

"I think I've got a hit on the vehicle."

"The lorry?"

Charlie nodded.

"Damn, I'm waiting for Patti to get back to me. Hang fire. Get all the evidence together, see if you can trace the vehicle et cetera. I'll be with you soon."

Charlie turned and walked away, but Katy called her back. She poked her head around the door again.

"Well done, Charlie, this is just the news we've been hoping for."

"Thought you might say that."

Her phone rang, and she snatched it up. "DI Katy Foster. How—"

"Cut the rest of the crap, it's me. Right, I have to ask if you're sitting down before I begin."

"Yes, sounds ominous. Give it to me."

"The reports are in, as you know, and I have to say some of them make interesting reading."

"Are you going to tell me what that is or keep me dangling?"

"Ooo…get you, Mrs Knickers-in-a-Twist."

"My knickers are just fine, thank you. Come on, Patti, I'm dying to frigging know what you're talking about."

"All righty, then. Hold on tight. The weapon, the gun that was used on Thatcham, or more to the point, the bullets we extracted from his body have matched a weapon on our system."

"Wow, okay. So the gun has been used during another crime. Do we know which one?"

"We do. Remember a few years ago there was a shootout with a couple of gangs in East London? Several fatalities, and I believe the rest of them were hauled in and banged up for their sins."

"Of course I remember. You're telling me we possibly missed a weapon?"

"Nope. What I'm telling you is that a weapon that was supposed to be locked away in your evidence room has somehow found its way back on the street again and into the hands of these thugs."

"Fuck, are you serious? How the hell does something like that happen?"

"You tell me," Patti said, her tone as high-pitched as Katy's.

Katy sighed, puffed out her cheeks and scratched her neck. "I need to get my hands on those reports and quickly, Patti. The chief will need to be informed of this. Jesus, we could be talking about a bent copper in our midst, at least, and possible police corruption, at most. Fuck, why me? Why did this jeffing thing have to land on my sodding desk?"

"Are you all right?"

"Hardly. My whole working world has just imploded before my very eyes. Why couldn't this have happened a few months ago when Lorne was bloody here? She could have dealt with the copper involved at the end of her career and ridden off into the sunset not giving two hoots about the frigging consequences. But no, it has to land on my sodding desk, opening me up for major effing flack. Sod it! I know that sounds selfish but..."

"It does not. It sounds like you're watching your back, which you always have to do being a copper. And yes, run it past Roberts, it'll ease the pressure on you. I'll send the reports through now. Good luck, Katy. You know I'm always around if you need moral support."

"Thanks, on both counts, Patti. Speak soon, I have things to do and people to see."

She ended the call and rushed out of the office. "Karen, will you get Graham and Stephen on the phone for me in a conference call? I have something major to tell them before they get to their locations."

"Will do."

A few seconds later, Karen motioned for Katy to join her. "Here's the boss now, guys."

"Graham and Stephen, I've just had word from the forensics that the weapon used on board the boat was obtained illegally."

"Not surprising, guv, considering who we're dealing with," Graham replied.

"Stop interrupting and let me damn well finish, man. This is important. The gun, it would appear, had been acquired from the secure evidence room at this station. Now, do you understand why I'm warning you?"

"Shit! How is that possible?" Graham asked.

"I don't know. There are too many connotations to go through right now. Just be careful out there."

"Thanks for the warning, guv. We'll ensure we're vigilant at all times," Stephen assured her.

Graham concurred. Katy ended the call and noted all the rest of the team's horrified expressions.

"Shit! Are you serious?" Charlie was the first to find her voice.

"Deadly. I need to run this past the chief, if only to cover our backs. I'll be right back."

*T*risha smiled the second Katy entered the room.

"Can I see him? It's an emergency," Katy said, grimly. The speed at which the adrenaline was pumping through her system was making her feel a little giddy.

"Sure, let me see for you." Trisha left her desk, knocked on her boss's door and entered the room. She reappeared within a few seconds and gestured for Katy to come in.

"Sorry to interrupt, sir. I have something very important that I need to discuss with you ASAP."

"Thanks, Trisha, that'll be all." Roberts dismissed his secretary and pointed at the chair opposite him. "Take a seat, Katy. What's so important?"

"Jesus, I don't know where to start. My head feels like it's been through ten rounds with Mike Tyson and is reverberating back and forth."

"Take a breath and start at the beginning."

"I can't, I need to get to the heart of the matter immediately. The fact is, sir, that I fear we have a bent copper scenario on our hands."

"That's quite a statement to expect me to digest without any accompanying facts. Why do you believe that, Katy?"

She spent the next few minutes recounting the conversation she'd had with Patti, ten minutes or so before.

"Okay, let's not overreact to the news. It might not be as bad as it seems."

"What? Did I hear you right? How can this not be bad, sir?"

"Let's begin an investigation into the allegation first and go from there."

Katy shook her head. "What allegation? It's nothing of the sort. The evidence is clear, what more do you need to go on? Someone has released a gun from this station and delivered it into the hands of criminals."

"I appreciate what you're saying, I truly do. However, we need to monitor the situation carefully before we go barging in with our size ten feet."

"Speak for yourself," she muttered, pissed off with what he was telling her.

"I can tell you're not happy about what I'm saying, but all I'm asking you to do is sit on the information for a day or two."

"Why? I can't see the point in that, sir. You know it's linked to my investigation and yet you're not prepared to do anything about it."

"I didn't say that. There are times when the evidence room is cleared of certain weapons."

"Well, that's bloody news to me. How? Where do they end up?"

"Now and then they're gathered together and disposed of. This might well be one of those occasions."

"If that's true, then I find it incredible to believe."

"They are usually disposed of carefully. I suppose, like everything, there could be slip-ups along the way."

Katy shook her head. "I'm inclined to stick with my notion, that we're dealing with a bent copper."

Roberts' expression turned sour. "Okay, let's see if my option is viable first, if only to save face. There should be a record of the weapons that have been disposed of. Let's check that and then go from there."

"I hate to ask, but can I leave that for you to sort out?"

"May I ask why?"

"Your seniority will speak volumes. If I go down there shouting the odds, well, it could cause a lot of friction, if you get what I mean."

He glanced at the mound of paperwork on the left-hand side of his desk. "As if I haven't got enough to do today."

"You and me both," Katy mumbled. "I have people to interview. They're being brought in now, as we speak."

"Go. Leave this to me."

Katy smiled and rose to her feet. "Thanks, boss, that's a load off my mind. Will you keep me updated?"

"Don't you go thinking you can wrap me around your little finger like your predecessor, Inspector."

Katy sniggered. "Sorry, I wouldn't dream of thinking anything of the sort, sir. Good luck in your mission."

"Thanks," he grumbled.

Katy closed the door behind her and released a long breath.

"Everything all right, Inspector?" Trisha asked.

"I think so. I'll let you know after I've fathomed out what just happened in there." She chuckled and left a confused Trisha behind and made her way back up the corridor to the incident room.

The news that greeted her rocked her to her core.

"We've got another one," Charlie announced.

"What? Another murder?"

Charlie nodded. "Jesus, tell me on the way. Do you have the details?"

Her partner waved a sheet of paper.

10

$\mathcal{K}$aty was pleased to see Patti and her team already at the scene when she and Charlie arrived. They slipped into their protective suits and joined the pathologist.

"Don't say it," Katy warned.

"I wasn't going to mention anything like fancy seeing you here. Sorry for being so predictable. Another crime scene to add to your tally."

"Don't tell me his car was stolen, too?"

"Yep. We've got a witness." Patti pointed out a young woman in a uniform, sitting on the edge of the kerb with a female constable comforting her.

"Who is she?"

"His girlfriend. They were setting off for work. He left the house first; she was delayed, seeing to the cat's needs. When she came out of the house, she found him lying there and his car gone."

"Sod it. I'll have a chat with her. How did he die?"

"My first impression would be that he was clobbered on the back of the head with a heavy object, maybe a metal bar."

"Then what?"

"They just kept beating and beating him until he took his last breath."

"What the fuck? For what? His damn car? I've had it with these guys. I'm determined to make this the last person they kill."

"How do you propose doing that, Katy?" Patti asked, intrigued.

"We've got two women on their way to the station, at least I hope they are by now. It's my intention to grill them and get the truth out of them."

"I take it they're connected to the murderers in some way."

"Yep, girlfriends of two of them, we think, well…according to their social media pages."

"Fair play to you. Right, we both have jobs to do. I need to get this young man examined and shifted, we're already attracting the rubber-neckers."

"We'll be back once we've spoken to her."

Together, Katy and Charlie walked over to the distraught woman. The PC remained seated and nodded a hello.

Katy produced her ID. "Hello, we're DI Katy Foster and DC Charlie Simpkins. I appreciate how distressing this has been for you, but are you up to talking to us?"

"I suppose so. Will it bring Ross back?"

Katy let out a ragged breath. "Sorry, no, it won't. However, the more you can tell us, the more likely it is that we'll capture the person responsible."

"I don't know if I can tell you anything. I didn't see what happened. I came out of the house and found him…lying there… covered in blood." She sobbed and added, "He didn't deserve this. Why would someone kill him?"

"Sorry, what's your name?"

"It's Vicki White, and that's my fiancé, Ross Samuels."

"Can you tell us what occupation Ross had?"

"Why?"

"It will give us some indication of where to look for possible clues."

"He's... he was a doctor at the hospital. The A&E department. I'm a nurse there. We were about to set off for work when this happened."

"Has Ross had any form of trouble in his life recently? Anyone had cause to have a go at him, possibly?"

"No. Never. He was a very friendly kind of bloke. Would rather help people than see them suffer. He was a doctor, for God's sake, that should tell you everything you need to know."

"I had to ask. I'm sorry. Can we call someone to come and sit with you?"

"The constable has rung my sister. She lives twenty minutes away, she should be here soon."

Katy glanced over her shoulder at the crowd increasing before her eyes. It sickened her to think of them treating this as some kind of horror show, which of course it was, but Vicki still had a right to her privacy. "Okay, that's good. Would you rather wait inside the house?"

"I'm not sure I can face going back in the house, the house I shared with Ross. All I want to do is curl up and die. The person who did this might as well have killed me as well, I can't go on without him. We were getting married in two weeks..." She broke down again.

Katy swallowed down the lump in her throat. "That's terrible, you have my condolences."

"I don't need them or want them. I want him...my Ross, the love of my life." Her hand shook as she pointed at her deceased fiancé.

"We'll get the justice you and Ross deserve, you have my word on that. Look, I really think you should go inside."

"I can't. I don't ever want to step inside that house again. His smell will be in every room. Reminders of him will be everywhere, I can't deal with any of this right now."

"I understand."

A car screeched to a halt, and a blonde-haired woman shot out of the vehicle and bent down in front of Vicki. She hugged her, and both women cried together while the three officers watched on. It was painful and tragic to witness.

Eventually, the newcomer released Vicki and got to her feet. "Who's in charge here?"

"That would be me, DI Katy Foster, and you are?"

"Sharon Knolls. Vicki is my sister. Do you know what happened? This is supposed to be one of the best areas on this side of town. This shouldn't have happened, not to Ross. This is too distressing for words."

"I understand how upset you must be, Sharon, we're doing our best to piece things together, but Vicki hasn't really told us much yet."

Vicki brushed the PC's arm off her shoulders and jumped to her feet. "I know nothing. I didn't see anything. What more can I tell you?"

Sharon hooked an arm around her sister's waist. "All right, calm down, there's no point in you upsetting yourself further, love."

"I need her to get her finger out and do something. Whoever did this has, and is, getting away. All she's intent on doing is standing around here asking dumb questions."

Katy held up her hands and backed up two paces. "We'll leave you to it. It wasn't my intention to cause you even more angst at a time like this. I suggested your sister goes inside, away from the glare of the onlookers."

"It's okay. I'll collect the cat and pack a bag for her and take her back to my place. Please, do what you can to ease her pain."

"You have my word. We'll ask the neighbours if they saw anything."

"Very well. Good luck. Come on, sis, let's get you in the car, and I'll do what's necessary inside the house." Sharon led her sister away and deposited her in the passenger seat of her Mini. Then she flew past them and into the house.

"Jesus. I can't deal with any more aggro. We need to frigging get these guys off the streets ASAP before I bloody lose my mind."

"Want me to start asking the crowd if they saw anything?" Charlie suggested.

"If you would. I'll try and hurry Patti along with the PM on this one, just to give Vicki a break."

On her way back to Patti, Katy received a call from Graham. "Hi, how did it go?"

"Just checking in to tell you Steve and I have got the two women. We're on our way back to the station."

"All right. What was their reaction? Any form of trouble?"

"One of them, Katrina Banks, appears a little subdued, bewildered even, and the other one, Alison Temple, kicked up a right fuss. Steve had to restrain her with cuffs."

"Damn, I really didn't want it to go down like that. They could be completely innocent in this. Never mind, what's done is done. Charlie and I are at another murder scene. A doctor was killed, and his Aston Martin was stolen."

"Shit! That's five bodies now."

"Seven counting our two guys, all in the space of a few days. This has to be the last one, we're going to have to up our game."

"We'll do our very best, boss. Are you going to be delayed?"

"Maybe. Get the women settled in an interview room, I'll be back as soon as I can. We're just finishing up here. See you soon." She ended the call and wound her way back to Patti. "The crowd is growing. Are you any closer to getting out of here?"

"Should be able to move in the next ten minutes or so. What is wrong with people? You'd think they'd show someone grieving more consideration, wouldn't you? Gawping twats. Excuse my aggression."

"That's not like you, Patti. I can understand you being pissed off, though. Sick shits. I'll see if uniform can disperse them, if not, I'll get them to move the cordon back several feet, if that will help."

"Great. As it stands, I'm feeling more than a little claustrophobic."

Katy marched over to the officer who had greeted her upon their arrival. "Let's see if we can move them back, let the pathologist and her team have some breathing space while they carry out their important roles."

"Will do, ma'am. Another ten feet?"

"If not more. Can't stand all this attention, it's not helping the fiancée much either."

"Leave it with me."

Charlie came towards her.

"Anything?" Katy asked.

"One man at the back said he saw four men travelling in the Aston Martin as it left the area. He'd been out walking the dog, was shocked to see the doctor lying on the ground."

"Did he bother to ring the police?"

"Nope, he told me someone had beaten him to it."

"Fair enough. Patti is almost done here. The fiancée is going back to her sister's house. Get uniform to continue the house-to-house, and we're out of here. I've just heard from Graham. He and Steve are on their way to the station with the two women. I'm keen to get them questioned."

"Give me five minutes to do the necessary and I'll be with you." Charlie trotted away again, a young recruit on a mission.

*I*t had been a whirlwind of a day so far. Katy had the start of a headache pounding at her temples. "I hate taking them but I'm going to have to shove a couple of paracetamols down my throat to get me through these two interviews."

"Sorry to hear it. I have some on my desk if you want some."

"I'm fine, I've got a supply in my drawer, next to a half bottle of brandy. I'm going to have to dig deep to resist the temptation to swill them down with it."

Charlie chuckled. "What do you want me to do?"

"While I dose myself up, can you ensure both women are comfortable? Make sure they've got a drink to hand and are aware of their right to have a solicitor present."

"Will do."

Katy trudged upstairs, each step booming through her body, her head feeling like a herd of elephants were playing football inside her skull. *Shit! Just what I need.*

After downing a couple of tablets and checking in with the rest of the team while she sipped a glass of water, Katy returned downstairs to face the first interviewee. Thankfully, by the time she reached Interview Room One, the pain had decreased significantly to a dull throb.

She entered the room to find a young woman in a brightly coloured tracksuit. Her blonde hair had bright-red streaks and was tied back in a ponytail. She glared at Katy and blew a bubble on the gum she was chewing.

Great, the epitome of a chav. Oh, what joy I have ahead of me.

Charlie introduced the woman as Alison Temple and her solicitor sitting alongside her as Miss Warren.

"Delighted to meet you both," Katy said, her tone light, hoping to get the interview off on the right note. The solicitor opened her mouth to speak but halted when Katy raised a finger, instructing her to wait. "DC Simpkins, will you do the honours for the recording? Thanks."

Charlie reeled off who was present in the room, and then Katy motioned for the solicitor to go ahead with what she was about to say.

"I'd like to know the purpose of this interview with my client, Inspector?"

"It's just a general enquiry, Miss Warren. Shall we press on?"

"If you insist." Miss Warren removed her pen from the slot in her clipboard and prepared to take notes, ignoring the glare her client was giving her.

Katy resisted the urge to chuckle at the indignation she spotted in Temple's expression.

"Miss Temple, perhaps we'll start with you telling us how you know Ray Thatcham."

Temple's face screwed up, and the intensity of her chewing increased. "Who?"

"Ray Thatcham," Katy repeated. "Come now, the name must mean something to you."

"Nah, never 'eard of him."

Katy frowned and scratched her chin. "How strange." She opened the manila folder she'd brought along with her and removed a copy of the bank statement Karen had highlighted for her. "Tell me, are those your account details?"

"How the hell should I know?"

Katy's blood boiled. "You don't know?"

"No," she bit back, the word laced with sarcasm.

"Odd. Do you mind checking for me?"

"How?"

"Is that your handbag beside you? Perhaps you have your cheque book inside."

"Nope, guess again. What's one of them anyway? I do all my banking online." Her gaze dropped to the floor, as if she'd opened her mouth and regretted the words which had freely tumbled from it.

"In that case, do you mind getting out your phone and opening up your bank app?"

"Can she do this?" Alison was quick to ask her solicitor.

"Give her what she wants. The sooner you do that the quicker we can get out of here."

She leaned down, swooped her medium-sized bag onto her lap and dug around inside the cavity to retrieve her mobile. "Do I have to?" she asked for clarification a second time.

Katy shrugged. "In all honesty, no, you don't *have* to, however, if you don't then I will have no alternative but to take a dim view of the situation and think you have something to hide."

"I ain't, I'm telling you."

"Open up the app," Miss Warren advised sternly.

Alison grunted and punched in her password. There was a brief delay while the information came through, and then she dropped her phone on the desk as if it had burned her fingers. "What the fuck? How did that get in there? Whoa...wait a minute, is someone setting me up? Who is this man you're talking about? I swear, I've never heard the name before. Shit! What the hell...?"

"Okay, let's take things slowly here. Are you telling me you had no idea those funds were in your account?"

"No, you have to believe me. It's a shock to see that amount sitting there."

"When was the last time you checked your account?" Katy asked.

"Last week sometime. Fuck, what does this mean? You haven't answered my question, who is this man?"

"Ray Thatcham lost his life three days ago."

"What? And you think I have something to do with it, is that it?"

She pushed her chair back, tipping it over as she stood and slammed her clenched fists on the table.

"Sit down, Miss Temple," Katy warned.

Aghast, the woman stared blankly at her solicitor. "Say something. Do something. I ain't being fitted up for no one."

"Do as the inspector said and take a seat, Miss Temple. Keep calm while we sort out this misunderstanding."

Alison righted the chair and plonked herself into it. She leaned back and folded her arms across her slim chest which was rising and falling rapidly due to her anxiety. "I need to get this sorted. I swear, I don't know how that got into my account."

"And you know what?" Katy said, "I believe you."

"Thank fuck for that. Tell me what's going on then."

"First of all, I need to check a few things with you. Such as who has access to your account."

"No one. If anyone got hold of my phone, they'd have a job getting into the app. My password is so weird even I have a job remembering it some days."

"Do you have a partner, Miss Temple?"

"Yeah, Stitch. Why?"

And there it was... "Stitch? Does he have a proper name, assuming Stitch is a he?"

"He is, I ain't one of those lesbos, if that's what you're getting at. I only know him as Stitch."

"And how long have you known your fella?"

"Three, maybe four months. Why? You think he has something to do with this?"

"I do. What does Stitch do for a living?"

"No idea. He told me never to ask."

"And that didn't arouse your suspicions at all?"

"Nah, I like sex, what can I say? I don't want the rest of the baggage that comes with a relationship. In that respect, we're two of a kind. It works well for both of us, and the sex is fantastic. Oops...sorry TMI, right?" She laughed.

She was the only one.

"The thing is, we believe your fella was involved in a serious crime a few days ago. We're very interested in speaking with him. Do you know where he is?"

"Nah, haven't seen him all week. What crime?"

"The murder of Ray Thatcham, the man who deposited that large sum of money into your account."

"Wait...what the...? I had nothing to do with no murder. I ain't taking the rap for it, if that's why you've dragged me in here." She faced her solicitor. "Don't just sit there, say something."

"Inspector, my client clearly has no notion of why those funds were deposited in her account. Why don't you issue a caution this time and let her go?"

"Let her off with a caution? A significant amount of money is deposited into her account the same day a man loses his life and you expect me to slap her on the wrist and release her? I don't think that's how it works, Miss Warren, do you?"

"Well, if you put it that way..."

"What? I had nothing to do with this. Here"—Alison picked up her mobile—"tell me where to transfer the money and I'll do it right away. I don't want it."

"We'll do that soon. Come on, Miss Temple, are you telling me your fella has access to your account and you knew nothing about it?"

"He must have. Maybe he saw a bank statement when it came through the post, I don't know. I usually leave them unopened in a pile in the kitchen, maybe he swiped one. Fuck, you have to believe me. I want no part of this. I didn't kill no one. I ain't taking the fall for this."

"In that case, we'd be willing to work with you."

"*Work* with me? I don't get you, how?"

"As I've already told you, we're very interested in speaking with Stitch. You must have a contact number for him, yes?"

"Yeah, I have. What about it?"

Katy passed her a pen and paper. "Give me his number."

"Now hold on a minute, if he's killed someone and I'm gonna give you his number, where the fuck does that leave me?"

"We'll protect you. The net is closing in on him and his gang," she lied. "But with your help we can get them off the streets sooner than we anticipated. Maybe when I tell you this it will help make up your mind. This week, your fella and his gang have killed seven people—five members of the public and two police officers. Do you really want to be connected with someone who has that on his CV?"

"Shit! No way. I didn't know." Tears spilled onto her cheeks, her rough exterior crumbling before Katy's eyes. "Please, help me. Tell me what to do. No, I don't want to get involved. I want to get away from here. I have family up north. Let me go to them."

"The first thing I need you to do is try to remain calm. We'll help you if you're willing to help us. Don't panic."

"I'll do anything. I want no part of this. It was only about the sex, I swear. We never went out or nothin'. I know nothin' about him."

"Where did you meet?"

"In a nightclub, I was out with the girls."

"And what? He came up to you and asked you out?"

Her cheeks flared up. "Umm…no, he took a shine to me. I was flattered, we had a quick shag in the men's loo, and the rest is history. He turns up at my gaff when he wants. It suits both of us, neither of us is keen on being at the other's beck and call."

"I see. So you haven't met any of his associates?"

"Not really. I saw one once. God, what am I saying? Katrina Banks and her fella and Stitch and I all went out one night."

"Hence the photos on your Facebook page?"

"You know about them? Have you been spying on me?"

"I wouldn't class it as spying, I'd call it more research than spying." Katy grinned.

"Typical of you lot to twist things. What happens next?"

"Once you've given us his contact details, we'll let you go, escort you back to your house so you can pack a bag and see you on your way."

She searched her phone, jotted down the information on the sheet of paper and slid it back to Katy. "There you go. What about the money?"

"I'll give you the account details, and we'll get the money transferred back to Mr Thatcham's account. That'll make things right with his estate then."

"I'm sorry this happened. Thanks for believing me. I would have been devastated if you'd blamed me and dragged me into it."

"We can tell you're innocent. See, the police aren't always ogres."

"Yeah, thanks, I appreciate it. Have you got the details for me? I want this money out of my account ASAP. I hate the thought of it being blood money."

Once the transfer had been made, Katy arranged for the woman to be escorted home. From there she'd pack a bag and travel up north to her relatives. She had assured Katy, when she'd seen her off at the main entrance, that Stitch didn't know where her family lived. Hearing that piece of news put Katy at ease. She'd feel guilty as all hell if Stitch found out Alison had been brought into the station and went after her with the intent to punish her for opening her damn mouth.

Katy didn't waste any time getting to grips with the next interviewee. Miss Warren was already seated at the table, along with Katrina Banks and Charlie. "Sorry to keep you. Would you start the recording, DC Simpkins?"

Her partner said the usual verbiage, and then Katy looked at the young brunette woman with overlapping front teeth and plump lips and said, "Here's the rub, Katrina, I need you to be honest with me."

"About what? I'm confused about why you've picked me up and brought me here."

"You were brought in for questioning regarding this." She flipped open the manila folder Charlie had transferred from the other room. "Would you mind explaining why one hundred thousand pounds was put in your account a few days ago?"

The woman's ruddy complexion evaporated to be replaced by one resembling her likelihood of seeing a ghost. "I...umm...I..."

"Yes, Miss Banks? We're all listening and intrigued to know. Spit it out. Oh, wait, before you try thinking up a plausible excuse, I have to tell you that Alison told us the truth."

Her eyes widened. "She did?"

"Yes. We know about Stitch and his mate."

Banks gasped. "Caves? Does she know where he is?"

"Sorry? I'm not with you. Care to explain what you mean by that statement?"

"Caves went missing…the day the money ended up in my account."

"Missing? How? When?"

"I don't know. I was at work when the money arrived. He'd warned me there was going to be a deposit made but didn't bother telling me how much. I was shocked, no, horrified to see that much in my account. I haven't seen him since."

"He hasn't tried to contact you?"

"No. His mobile is just ringing out and then going into voicemail. I'm really worried about him."

"May I ask why? Apart from the obvious, him not being in touch. What I meant was, do you have a reason to be concerned about his whereabouts?"

"Yes and no."

Katy raised an eyebrow. "Are you going to tell me or are you expecting me to guess?"

"He's always in danger. That's why he told me he was going to try and get a large sum in the next few days, if the opportunity arose."

"Danger? In what way? With his job?"

"Yes." She sighed and wrung her hands. "We've been together around six months now. He only broke the news to me about what job he does a few months back. I've been living on the edge ever since."

"May I ask why?"

"Because of the danger."

"What job did he tell you he was doing?"

"He's in a gang. The boss is super demanding. I begged him to leave, to find a better job. He went ballistic, told me to mind my own business and that he would leave when the time was right. That was a few weeks ago. He saw me last week and said he and Stitch had come up with a scheme and if things panned out the way they'd planned they could both be rolling in it within a few days."

"And that's all he told you, nothing more?"

"No. I swear. I got a call after the money had landed in my account and haven't heard a bloody peep out of him since."

"How did he describe his job to you?"

"He told me his boss was in the import and export business, high-value items, elite customers, that type of thing."

"I see. Did he tell you where he worked?"

"No. One day he let it slip that a meeting took place in a warehouse. He said the boss was livid about someone screwing up his plans and he was about to punish the tosser. His words not mine, sorry."

Katy waved a hand. "It doesn't matter. Do you think that has anything to do with the money being deposited into your account?"

"I don't know. Can't you help me to find him?"

"We'll do our best. When did he go missing?"

"On Tuesday, I think. Yes, it was definitely Tuesday. I'm worried something really bad has happened to him. He hasn't been happy in his job for a while. Kept saying he had a sense of imminent danger. Please, you have to help me."

"Imminent danger to himself?"

"Yes, at least, I think that's what he meant. He clammed up after I showed how concerned I was for his safety. He assured me that he had everything in hand and that I wasn't to worry about anything, and then…he went missing. Why wouldn't I be bloody worried about him?"

"Is it possible that he might be hiding somewhere?"

She shrugged. "Anything is possible, but I'm sure he would have told me what his intentions were… He loves me and I love him. He's trying to make a better life for himself and for me, hence the money."

"Ill-gotten-gained money, you mean."

She heaved out a sigh. "Whatever. If you play with the sharks, sometimes you have to sink your teeth into the huge chunk of bait."

"Okay, I suppose. Have you got a photo of Caves?"

She removed her phone from her denim jacket and scrolled through. Her eyes lit up when she found his photo and passed it over to Katy. "Handsome, isn't he?"

"Not my cup of tea, but I can sort of see the attraction. You like your men with muscles bigger than a bulldog, I see."

"I do. You know where you are with a man who takes care of himself."

Katy handed her the phone back. "Is that right?"

"Yes."

"I have some news that I believe you will find shocking in that case."

Katrina's eyes narrowed. "What type of news?"

"The worst kind. I have reason to believe your boyfriend is guilty of killing several people this week."

"*What*? I don't believe you. He isn't the type."

Katy inclined her head. "I fear you don't really know the man at all. This week alone there have been seven murders in this area, all carried out by a certain gang. We have it on good authority it's the same gang your fella belongs to."

She shook her head, her mouth opening and shutting as the words failed to come. Eventually, she found her voice. "This can't be true. Oh God, what if something serious has happened to him? Seven people… no, don't tell me he's one of the dead?"

"He's not, however, two police officers were caught up in the battle. Sadly, they lost their lives on Tuesday."

"Battle? Are you telling me one of your officers has killed him?"

"I didn't say that. Maybe battle was the wrong term. How about tussle? From the CCTV footage we've seen of the incident, our boys didn't fire, but either Caves or Stitch did, hence the officers both being killed."

"I'm sorry about that." And she seemed it.

"What can you tell me about Thatcham, the man who paid the money into your account?"

"I didn't know him personally. But Caves said he'd gone against the boss's wishes and the knives were out, so to speak. Don't tell me he lost his life through a stabbing?"

"Umm…maybe. I can't divulge that information just yet, not until I've had the PM—sorry, the post-mortem—results back. So, what can you do to help me? Caves is on the missing list, and I need to know why Thatcham, his girlfriend and two police officers lost their lives plus three others. The more you can tell me at this stage the better. At the moment, all we appear to be doing is going around in circles." Katy realised she shouldn't have been so open with the woman, but she felt there was no other option open to them. It was imperative to understand how this gang ticked, and if there was a way for her and her team to stop them taking any more lives, and expensive cars into the bargain, she'd grab it with both hands.

"I'm sorry, I really don't know that much. He told me when he was going on a job but not what it entailed. I'm appalled he killed people. I thought the gang were probably into drugs...oh dear, I'm not explaining myself properly, am I? How does that make me look, saying that I'm prepared to put up with him dealing and overseeing drug trafficking? And yet..."

"Drug trafficking? Is that what their business involves? Okay, let me run this past you. Three of the victims had their expensive cars stolen. Can you shed any light on that setup?"

"No, Caves didn't hint at anything like that. I'm sorry, I would tell you if he had. Look, I wish I could help, the fact is, I can't. Can you help me find him? I know that's asking a lot, I just don't know where to turn next."

"All I can tell you is that we'll keep an eye open for him during the rest of our investigation. Apart from that, I'd suggest you register him as a missing person."

"I thought about that. Okay, I'll do it. Is there anything else you need to ask me?"

"The boss, does he have a name?" Katy asked, chancing her arm.

Katrina contemplated the question and tucked a stray strand of hair behind her left ear. "I'm trying to think. He really didn't talk about him much. I got the impression if he could walk away he would do it in a heartbeat."

"Please, try and think. It could give us the turning point we need in the case. We're desperate to rid the streets of these killers before they take another life. Of course, that could have already happened."

Katrina stared at her long and hard. "You're talking about Caves, aren't you?"

Katy hitched up her shoulder. "Possibly. I hate to say it, but in my experience, gang members rarely go missing unless something dreadful has happened to them."

She shook her head in disbelief, and fresh tears escaped her eyes. "No, don't say that. I refuse to give up on him."

"Understandable. Please, try and think of the leader's name."

Katrina's gaze drifted to the corner of the room, and her eyes narrowed. She closed them as if willing the information to come forward. Slowly, her gaze returned to Katy, and a slight smile drew her lips apart. "I think I can remember what it is."

Katy smiled, enticing the woman to set the name free.

"It begins with an A, either Andrews...no, that doesn't sound right now I've said it out loud. Anders..." She clicked her fingers. "Anderton, yes, that's it. Don't ask me his first name, though. Will that help you?"

"It might. Can you think of anything else? Where he's based? Does he live in London, or perhaps on the outskirts? Anything at all?"

Rubbing her hand across her face, the young woman sighed and shook her head. "I'm sorry. I've done my best for you."

"Don't worry. We'll see where that leads us. We're thankful for you taking the time to speak to us. We'll get the money transferred and then what will you do? Go home?"

"I don't know." She held her hand out flat in front of her, and it trembled. "I'm a nervous wreck. What if they're watching me and they find out I've been speaking to you? What then? I could be in deep shit, couldn't I?"

"Would you like me to see if we have a safe house for you to stay at until we've captured the gang?"

Katrina gasped again. "You'd do that for me? Even though I've barely given you anything to go on?"

"Nonsense, you've given us a name. It's up to you. I can ask the question, or you can take the risk and head home. Do the gang know where you live?"

"I doubt it. What am I saying? How do I know? Caves might have told them in passing. I know, that's probably my mind working overtime. Please, yes, I'd like somewhere to stay for the next day or two, if that's all right with you?"

"It is. It's the least we can do. Hang tight for a few minutes. I'll make a call and get back to you soon."

"Thank you."

"Do you need me any more?" Miss Warren gathered her notebook and slotted it into her satchel.

"I don't think so. I'll show you out. Do you need anything, Katrina? I might be half an hour to an hour."

"A drink and a sandwich, if that's possible. I missed out on breakfast this morning," she replied sheepishly.

"No problem. DC Simpkins, can you deal with that for me?"

Her partner nodded.

Katy escorted the solicitor to the main entrance, shook her hand, and then ran up the stairs two at a time to the incident room. Breathlessly, she said, "I think we've got a lead. During the research, has anyone stumbled across the name Anderton?"

"No, why's that, boss?" Graham asked.

"The girlfriend of one of the thugs who killed the four people on the boat, his name is Caves, she's pretty sure that's the name of the bloke who runs the gang. By the way, she also told me that Caves has gone missing. She hasn't laid eyes on him since that incident occurred."

"Okay, what do you need us to do?" Graham asked, acting as the spokesperson for the team.

"Keep digging. How are we doing with the list of Range Rovers? Search that for a possible Anderton. The girlfriend couldn't tell me where this bloke is based. I'm taking a punt that it's within the city limits, just because of where the crimes have been committed. Also, we need to check the import and export businesses operating in the London area. She's under the impression he runs one of those and sneaks drugs into the country that way."

"Wasn't Thatcham an importer and exporter?" Karen chipped in.

"Too right. Try to obtain a list of contacts for the business. Ring his partner, see if he's willing to oblige. If not, chase up that damn warrant. I've let that slip, we should've had that by now, shouldn't we?"

"I'm on it. I should've chased it up myself, you've had enough on your plate," Karen replied.

"Nonsense, I'd rather not go down the blame game route, let's just get it sorted. I need to make a call. I've promised Katrina a place in a safe house after the information she's divulged. Did I say her boyfriend has gone missing? I can't ruddy remember. My sodding mind is racing faster than a Formula One car."

"You did," Steve said. "Want me to get you a coffee, boss?"

"Thanks, that'd be great. The caffeine might help steady the ship. I'll be in my office." She trotted through the doorway and took a deep breath. Her heart was trying to play catch-up with her mind. She flung herself into her chair and picked up the phone to call one of her contacts. "Ah, Des, it's Katy Foster. How are you fixed for properties at the moment?"

"Hi, Katy. You're in luck, I've just had a couple become vacant in the last two days. We're in the process of getting them cleaned up now. What do you need?"

"Brilliant. I can breathe a little easier, then. I've got a young woman who could do with laying low for the next two to three days."

"Alone?"

"Yes. A flat will do. Nothing special."

"I've got something that fits the bill. I'll chase up the cleaners. Can you give me twenty minutes?"

"Sure. I really appreciate it, Des. I owe you a pint next time I see you at the pub."

"I'll hold you to that."

Katy ended the call as Steve entered the office.

"You look as though you could do with this. Want me to source a biscuit as well?"

"Are you sucking up to me for a reason?"

He chuckled. "Not at all. And there was me thinking you were a good judge of character, boss."

"I am. What gives?"

"I swear, all innocent on my part. I'll get back to it."

"You do that. Thanks for the drink."

Finally, Katy received the return call from Des around forty-five minutes later. He apologised for the delay and gave her the address of a flat in the East End. "Thanks, mate, I'm so grateful to you. I'll get uniform to drop her over there now if one of your team can meet them at the address."

"Absolutely. Glad I could be of service. Speak soon."

She ended the call, left her office and ran back downstairs where she spoke to Mick on reception who offered to supply two officers, complete with Tasers, to escort Katrina Banks to the safe house, which was a relief and a severe weight off her mind. Katrina was equally relieved when Katy shared the news which had been anxiously awaited.

After placing Katrina in the back of a squad car, Katy and Charlie headed back to the incident room. The team had their heads down, clacking keyboards, the dominant sound in the room until Graham shouted, "Yes."

"Something positive, I hope, Graham," Katy called across the room.

"I hope you don't mind, boss, I sort of went off on a tangent and decided to do some digging of my own."

"Regarding? We're all keen to hear."

"I had a brainwave. Well, maybe that's a touch over the top. Let's just call it a suspicion, how about that?"

"Whatever it's called, get on with it, Graham, my patience has been getting thinner all day, and I'm close to my limit now at four in the afternoon."

"Sorry. Right, I was wondering how the gang could have possibly known about the vehicles and where to find them, so I rang my mate in forensics to ask him if he had an inkling."

"And what did your mate have to say for himself?" Katy asked, crossing her arms and resisting the temptation to tap her foot.

"He said that most cars of value are usually fitted with a GPS system, in case the cars are stolen at any time."

Katy cupped her chin with her right hand. "Crap, I thought about that, I even asked Ethan Johnson's staff if he had one on board, and then it slipped my mind to chase it up. Okay, ignoring that for a moment, how can we tell if the other cars had a system when all the owners have been killed?"

"Exactly, that could be their motive for killing them right there and then. The gang probably disabled the system right away, preventing the information transmitting to the GPS firm tracking the cars."

"I think you might be onto something. Roberts' suggestion might play a part in this, too. Maybe the gang drove the cars on the back of a lorry and then dismantled the tracker. Contact all the relatives concerned, see if they're aware of the tracker and if they can give you a name of the firm involved, if you would? I don't have to caution you to tread carefully, do I? They're grieving relatives."

"I'll be gentle with them, boss. Trust me." He bared his glistening white teeth in a grin.

It turned out to be Ross Samuels' girlfriend, Vicki White, who was the one to confirm the name of the business involved.

"Are you up for this, Charlie?" Katy asked en route to the firm's business address.

"Of course. I have to say, if they're guilty then I'm pretty shocked about it. Some security, eh? You put your trust in a firm like this and end up six feet under."

"Yeah, seems more than a little harsh, doesn't it?"

They continued the journey in silence, Katy wrapped up in her own thoughts as to why someone could be driven to do such a thing.

Golden Security's office was situated on a trading estate. The office was the shop front to a huge warehouse.

"Looks interesting. Got your pepper spray handy? I don't usually, but I think I'll take my Taser for this visit."

"I don't blame you."

They entered the office to find a young woman in her early twenties manning the front desk. Katy and Charlie flashed their warrant cards.

"We'd like to speak to the person in charge. Thanks," Katy said.

"May I ask why?"

"It's a personal matter."

"I'll see if Mr Harvey has time to see you. He's an exceptionally busy man."

"I'm sure. And we're exceptionally busy women, so if you don't mind hurrying things along a little."

She flew out of her chair. "Sorry, yes. I won't be long."

The receptionist was actually gone around five minutes, which seemed a tad excessive to Katy. "I hope they're not hiding evidence in there."

"Possibly," Charlie replied.

Katy inched towards the door the receptionist had entered, and Charlie followed. A man in a white shirt appeared at the end of the hallway. Katy smiled. The man frowned and disappeared back into the room he'd come out of.

"I'm getting a bad feeling about this," Katy mumbled.

"I'm inclined to agree with you. Want to burst into the room? I think we'd be within our rights."

"Let's hold fire for a few moments longer."

With that, the young receptionist appeared once more. "Oh, you're there. Okay, sorry for the delay. Mr Harvey was on an important call, and I couldn't interrupt him."

"For a second there we thought you'd forgotten about us. Thanks, he's free now, I take it?"

"Yes, come through. Can I get you a drink?"

"No thanks."

They followed the woman up the hallway and into a large window-less office. No, that wasn't quite true, there was a skylight at the far end, flooding the area with the sun's rays.

The gentleman behind the desk stood as they entered. "Sorry to keep you. I was talking with a client who had a list of a hundred questions to go through."

"No harm done."

"I'm Brian Harvey, I own this firm. How can I help?" He motioned for Katy and Charlie to take a seat and nodded to the receptionist to leave them.

"I'm DI Katy Foster, and this is my partner, DC Charlie Simpkins. It's very kind of you to see us at short notice, we appreciate how busy you are. We're hoping you'll be able to answer some questions regarding your products."

He retook his seat, and Katy and Charlie sat opposite him.

"If I can help, I surely will. What do you need to know?"

"We're a bit naïve as to how your system works. Would you care to enlighten us?"

"What's there to tell? We offer our clients peace of mind when they have one of our systems fitted to their cars. Customers only tend to come to us if they've spent around fifty grand on a car."

"I see. Do you advertise your services anywhere, or do most clients come to you via word of mouth?"

"We advertise in all the trade magazines. Plus, we offer the garages in the area a hefty bonus if they suggest adding one of our systems to the cars at the point of sale."

"Ah, right."

"Is there a specific reason why you want to know this?" Harvey asked, his head tilting.

"We're investigating a few crimes in the area, and your firm's name cropped up during the investigation."

His brow knitted. "I'm not liking the sound of that. Our name was linked to a few crimes? May I ask what type of crimes and how they have led you to my door?"

Katy inhaled a large breath. "The thing is, Mr Harvey, this week alone, three valuable cars have been stolen. We know at least one of those cars had a tracking system on it which you supplied."

"Goodness me. This is the first I've heard about it. If there was a problem, I find it incredulous to believe that the owners wouldn't have contacted us right away."

"Ah, that would be difficult as all three owners of the vehicles have since died."

"What? Since died? As a result of their cars being stolen, is that what you're telling me?"

"Yes. Two died at the scene and one later in hospital due to the injuries he sustained during the robbery."

He shook his head in disbelief and ran a hand through his cropped hair. "I'm so sorry. I don't know what else to say. What can I do to help?"

"I wondered if you could check to see if all the cars were registered with you for a start."

"Of course. Let me get the manifest."

He walked the length of the large room and returned carrying a folder. "Can I have the names of the owners?"

Katy reeled the names off one by one. Each time, Harvey tutted and nodded in affirmation.

"Oh dear, yes, all three of those men were registered with us. What does that mean?" he asked, his eyes darting nervously between Katy and Charlie.

"I don't know. I was hoping you'd tell us, sir," Katy said.

His clenched fist stabbed at his chest. "No. You can't believe I had anything to do with this?"

Katy shrugged. "Unless you can offer another solution then we'll have no other alternative but to believe that, Mr Harvey."

"What? Why? I've never, ever in my life been investigated by the police. I'm above reproach. My business is genuine. I have all my paperwork intact. My goodness, what else can I say to make you believe me?" His voice became high-pitched within seconds.

"Are you telling us that you're willing to work with us on this, Mr Harvey?"

"Yes, for the love of God, my reputation is at stake here. If word gets out about you being here it could cripple my business. I'm willing to do anything to prevent that happening. Just tell me what you need."

"I'm glad you're willing to cooperate with us. If, as you say, you know nothing about these crimes, we need to know if one of your staff could be culpable."

"Possibly, however, I'd be cut up to learn any of them were behind anything as sinister as what you're suggesting."

"How many staff do you have working on site?"

"Eight at the moment, we're interviewing for two more engineers."

"May I ask why?"

"Just because our workload has increased by twenty percent over the past few months, and they say there's no money around. Well, I can tell you, the car industry is thriving."

"And of the eight members of staff, how many have been loyal employees and worked here for years?"

"Most of them. We've been up and running since twenty-ten. I obtained a huge contract from a local premium garage so was able to set up a large workforce from the outset."

"And you trust your staff?"

"They wouldn't be on the payroll if I didn't, I assure you."

"Has anyone mentioned they're struggling to you?"

"I don't understand, in what respect?"

"Perhaps financially? Maybe they're in debt and that's led them to doing things out of character, like stealing the cars."

"I doubt it. I can't believe you're suggesting such a thing. I've always had a high regard for my staff. This is incredible. I can understand your line of questioning but..."

"Then we're up shit creek as they say, if you'll excuse my language. We don't know where to look. The cars were stolen, and the owners lost their lives while trying to defend their vehicles, that's our belief. What about your contacts, do you know of anyone likely to be involved with anything that could be labelled as dodgy?"

"Goodness me, what do you take me for? If I got a whiff of any form of corruption, I'd dob the person in to the police, I can assure you."

Katy released a heavy sigh. "Then I don't know what to think. I need a resolution and I genuinely have no idea where to turn next. Would you mind if we had a word with your staff before we leave?"

"Go for it. Want me to arrange a room where you can interview them? At the end of the day, I want this issue resolved as much as you do."

"Glad to hear it. I wish all bosses were as flexible as you, sir."

"Give me five minutes to make the arrangements." He strode out of the room, determination in his stance.

"Do you believe him?" Charlie asked, glancing over her shoulder at the door.

"I think so. Don't you?"

"Yes and no. I believe someone here is responsible. It's too much of a coincidence otherwise, right?"

"Yep. I agree."

The door opened, and Harvey came back into the room. "If you'd like to come this way."

He showed them through the warehouse to a storeroom out the back. A table with three chairs had been pulled into the middle of the room.

"I set up this area for you, will it suffice?"

"It will, thanks for your help. Can we see the men in seniority, if that's possible?" Katy asked.

Harvey nodded. "If you insist. I'll send the supervisor in first."

A slim gentleman in blue overalls entered not long after. "Hi, I'm Derek, the supervisor around here. The boss told me to drop by and see you."

"Hi, Derek, I'm DI Foster, and this is DC Simpkins. Take a seat, we promise not to keep you long."

"Thanks. What's this about?"

"Well, we're making general enquiries, concerning four cases we're working on. Very serious cases, and the evidence has led us to this facility."

Derek cocked his head and seemed perplexed by Katy's statement. "How so?"

"First of all, I need to know if you've heard on the grapevine about any high-priced, valuable cars being stolen."

He let out a short laugh. "No, sorry about that. I was just thinking, serves them right for not having one of our trackers fitted."

"The trouble is, one of your systems was fitted to each of the cars."

"Holy shitballs on fire, seriously?"

"Yep. Which is why we're here, to try and get to the bottom of our dilemma."

He shrugged. "Sorry, I can't help you."

"Well, we believe someone knows something around here. Help us out if you will. Can you think of anyone who has been acting suspiciously at work lately?"

"No, not that I've noticed. Hold on, yes, now you've come to mention it, Aaron Salter did something out of character last week."

Katy raised an eyebrow, and Charlie wrote the information down in her notebook.

"Care to share with us what that was about?" Katy asked.

"From what I can remember, one of the other guys saw him fiddling with one of the GPS systems, doing something that could disable it at the drop of a hat."

"And that's something out of the ordinary, I take it?"

"Too right. It's supposed to be an infallible system. Secure, not to be messed with."

"And what was his reason for tampering with it?"

"He said he was only testing it. It's just not something we do."

"What, test your equipment?"

"No, that came out wrong. We don't go down the line of disabling the equipment. What would be the point in us doing that?"

"I really don't profess to know the ins and outs of having a GPS system in a car, it's not something that has crossed my mind to have fitted over the years."

"I think every person who drives a car should have something similar fitted, but there again, I might be biased."

"So you reprimanded Salter, and that was the end of the discussion?"

"That's right. He said he was testing something out and then put it aside to get on with his work. Therefore, I didn't feel the need to tackle him about the subject again."

"I see, and what's his work ethic been like ever since? Have you had any cause to question it again?"

"Nope, although now you've raised the subject, he has been a little withdrawn for a few days. You think he has something to do with this?"

"We don't know. We'll speak to him next, if that's okay with you?"

"Too right. It would be good to know what's going on with him."

"Perhaps you can give us a bit of background on him first?"

"Such as?"

"How long he's worked here. Where he worked before. A bit about his personal life, such as if he's married or not, that type of thing."

"I'll do my best. He's been here from the get-go, since the business was set up. I can't recall off the top of my head where he worked before, the boss will be able to fill that part in for you, or Salter himself, of course. He's married to Lorraine. I don't think they have kids yet. Word is they're trying to have a family."

That piece of information sparked Katy's interest. "As in, it hasn't happened naturally and they're seeking other ways, such as IVF perhaps?"

He held his hands up. "Hey, I like to keep my nose out of other people's business. We're far too busy to engage in idle gossip around here. Anyway, it's not the done thing for blokes to talk about the nitty-gritty of conceiving a child. We tend to leave that to our womenfolk. All we're interested in is the production of the end product, if you know what I mean?"

"I understand. Has he been turning up for work on time?"

"Yep, never any doubts about his time-keeping."

"What about at the end of his shift, does he hang around or shoot off home?"

"Most of the lads go straight home, but the odd couple tend to have a sneaky pint at the pub. I'm not sure if he's one of them, though."

Katy pressed on. "Has he fallen out with any of the other team members recently?"

"Nope. He's a fairly placid chap. Tends to keep his head down most of the time and just get on with things. The same as the other guys. We're lucky we have a conscientious team here. Not sure every factory can say the same, especially these days."

"Okay. In that case, I think I've heard enough. Can we speak to him next?"

"If you're finished with me, I'll go and fetch him."

Katy nodded as he stood and walked out of the room.

"What are you thinking? IVF treatment, and he's struggling to find the funds to pay for the treatment?" Charlie suggested.

Katy smiled. "Sums it up perfectly. You're obviously thinking the same."

"Yes."

"Either way, if this gang are forcing him to do something against his will, I'm thinking he's not going to be pleased to see us, so be prepared."

The door opened, and a younger man entered, also in blue overalls with the logo of the business emblazoned on the top pocket. "You wanted to see me?" He stood by the desk.

Katy sensed he was going to refuse to take a seat. "If you'd like to sit down, Mr Salter."

"I'm all right standing," he snapped.

"As you wish. I'd better tell you who we are. I'm DI Katy Foster, and this is DC Charlie Simpkins."

"And? What does this have to do with me?"

"Is there something upsetting you, Mr Salter?"

"No, should there be?"

"It's just that I'm getting the impression you're not keen to talk to us."

"I'm not thrilled about being dragged in here away from my busy work schedule, if that's what you mean?"

"Any particular reason why you're not too happy about seeing us, Aaron?"

"I've said, I have a busy day ahead of me."

"Take a seat, this is important."

He grunted, flopped into the chair and automatically put up the defences by crossing his arms.

Katy pinned a smile in place. "Do you have anything you want to get off your chest?"

"In what respect?"

"Telling us what these people have over you, for instance."

He glared at her. "You're talking in damn riddles. What people?"

"Come on now. Don't make this harder than it needs to be."

He shrugged and continued to hold her gaze with his own. "Haven't got the foggiest what you're talking about."

"The gang. Your boss seems to think there's something bothering you, and we're investigating several murders. Care to fill in some of the gaps for us?"

Salter did something Katy hadn't anticipated. He tipped his chair back and ran for the door. Charlie was the quickest to react. She sprinted after him and even managed to reach the door ahead of him. Pepper spray in hand, she raised it to his face.

"Don't make me use it," she shouted.

Even Katy flinched at the aggression in Charlie's tone. She joined her partner and grabbed hold of Aaron's arm. "Sit down, don't make me slap the cuffs on you."

He shook his head. "You don't understand."

"Enlighten us." Katy led the man back to the table.

He shook his head, the momentum increasing as he appeared to be battling his conscience.

"Tell us, help us to understand what's going on, Aaron."

His gaze dropped to his wringing hands. "I can't, they'll…"

"Who will do what, Aaron? Come on, tell us, we can help."

"No police. They warned me not to contact you."

"Who did? The gang?"

He glanced up, pinning Katy with his vivid green eyes. "They're dangerous."

"I don't doubt that. What are they up to? We know it's something big, what we haven't managed to figure out yet is what they have over you."

He turned to look at the wall, and then his gaze rose to the ceiling. "I can't risk it."

"Risk what? What type of hold have they got over you?"

"It should be over soon. The next few hours and…"

"What should be? The cars, where are they heading, Aaron?"

"I can't tell you…they'll…"

Katy sighed as things slotted into place. "It's your wife, isn't it? They have her, don't they?"

He nodded. Katy sensed that if he said the words out loud, he'd possibly put another nail in her coffin.

"I'm sorry to hear that. Look, if you work with us, we can help you and your wife out of this predicament."

"I can't, they warned me what would happen if I blabbed. Don't force me to do this. I love my wife. By keeping quiet I'll be saving her life. If I tell you everything, well…they'll find out and kill her. I couldn't live with knowing that I caused her death."

"There are ways we can help without putting your wife in danger, Aaron. Work with us, please?"

"I can't. Anyway, it'll all be over tonight."

"Why? I repeat, where are the cars heading?"

"Abroad. To Saudi Arabia."

"Do you know how they're being shifted?"

"By boat. No, I've said enough already."

"You haven't, give us more. Come on, you really think these ruthless men are going to live up to the promise they've made to you once the transfer has gone through?"

"They wouldn't…they can't go back on their word. I've done everything that was asked of me."

"Aaron, I'm not sure if you're aware of what this gang has carried out this week in order to obtain the cars, so I'd like to let you in on that."

He shook his head.

"To date, they have killed five members of the public and two police officers. Does that sound like people you can put your trust in?"

"Shit! I didn't know. Those people died because of what I did. I won't be able to live with myself."

"If the work you did was done under duress then we can help you if the case goes to court."

"I can't be held responsible, can I?"

"If you see the light, as they say, then we can have a word with the Crown Prosecution Service, tell them you were forced to give the gang the information, but only if you help us."

"I'll do anything—not for my benefit, no, I couldn't give a toss what happens to me, but Lorraine needs to be rescued. Can you do that?"

"If you provide us with the information, then yes, we'll do our very best to rescue her and to help you in the process. What do you know?"

He swallowed hard. "Everything is in place now. All the cars are due to be delivered overnight."

"Where are they leaving from? What time?"

"You have to understand that they haven't divulged the information to me. I overheard one of the goons when I went to see the top man."

"Wait. You know who is running the operation?"

"Yes. Robert Anderton. I don't know much else about him, sorry. Only that he's ruthless when crossed."

"And you've been to his house? Place of work? Which?"

"A warehouse the gang use. Yes, I was taken there by one of his heavies."

"Can you tell us where that is?"

"No, they blindfolded me, didn't want to run the risk of me calling the police, I suppose."

"That's a shame. You've got no idea where that is? While you were there, perhaps you saw a local landmark that would help us identify the area."

"I don't recall. They didn't take the blindfold off until I was inside the building then secured it in place when they returned me to the car."

"So, let's run through the part you played in this scheme. How did they make contact with you?"

"I'm not sure. I think it was through a friend of a friend. They picked me up last week. Offered me a six-figure sum which I turned down. On Saturday, I went out fishing with a friend, and when I came home I found a note saying they'd taken Lorraine and to contact them ASAP if I wanted her back. I rang the number they gave me, and they insisted either I work with them or I say goodbye to Lorraine. What could I do but accept? I said I would, providing they didn't harm her."

"Did they give you proof of life?"

"Are you asking if they've delivered a finger or something? Then no, they haven't."

"Not really. Have you spoken to her since she disappeared? Have you had anything along those lines to tell you that she's still alive?"

"No. I suppose I just took their word for it. Was I wrong to do that? What if they've hurt her…or worse still…what if she's…?"

"Don't think about that for now."

"It's hard not to, I've hardly slept all week. I've thought about nothing else. Shit, and now you're telling me these thugs have killed the owners of the cars I've helped them to steal? Fucking hell, what a mess. I don't see a way out. What if Lorraine is already dead? What then? How will I be able to go on?"

"Try not to dwell on it. Going back to the delivery of the vehicles."

"They're being shipped out by container from the Port of London this evening."

"What time?" Katy asked, her excitement notching up a level.

"Ten, I think. It was a mumbled response I heard, so don't quote me on it. It's definitely the right area, though, so you might want to conduct your own investigation into that."

Charlie scribbled down the information. "Going to Saudi Arabia, yes?"

"Correct. You know they have the money over there."

"So the cars were stolen to order, is that it?"

"Yes, Anderton is a local businessman, exports and imports. Don't ask me the name of his company. He takes pride in obtaining items that others can't."

"But used cars? Why wouldn't the Saudis go to the manufacturers and buy them direct?"

"Don't ask me. Maybe Anderton steals them, clocks the cars and then ships them out."

"Possibly, that part would make sense."

Salter sighed. "Please, I've given you all the information I have, we're wasting time."

"One last thing. You haven't told us when they said they'd be releasing Lorraine."

"I'm expecting a call this evening. I presume it will come through once the ship has left the dock. I'll be on tenterhooks until then. Please, I'm begging you not to take any risks with my wife's life."

"Don't worry. We won't. Okay, I think you should leave work now. What time are you due to knock off?"

"In half an hour. Sorry, I'd rather stay here, stick to my usual routine, just in case someone is keeping an eye on me. Shit, don't tell me you've turned up in a cop car?"

"We have, an unmarked one. Okay, stay here. If they make contact with you, I need you to ring me straight away, okay?" Katy slid a card across the table.

"I will. I'm sorry, I didn't mean to get those people killed."

"It was extenuating circumstances, you're not to blame."

"I think you're being kind. Good luck, please be careful, don't put my wife's life in jeopardy."

"We won't, you have my word. Thanks for having the courage to be honest with us."

"I don't feel courageous in the slightest. In fact, I feel like shit for the role I've played in all of this."

"Don't beat yourself up." Katy rose from her chair, followed by Charlie and Aaron.

Together they left the room.

"I'm not going to say anything to your boss, that can wait for another day." Katy smiled at Aaron and patted his forearm. "Go back to work and act as if nothing has happened. We'll make up an excuse for our early departure."

"Thanks for your understanding, Inspector. I'm not sure every copper in your position would have reacted the same way."

"There are always two sides to every story, Mr Salter. Take care, we'll be in touch soon."

They parted, and Katy and Charlie headed back to the owner's office.

The receptionist gave the all-clear for them to enter the room. "He's expecting you, told me to tell you to go straight in."

Katy gave her the thumbs-up and walked into the room.

"Ah, how are things going with the staff?" Mr Harvey asked, motioning for them to take a seat.

Katy held up a hand, declining his offer. "We managed to speak to a couple of people. Unfortunately, we've been called away on an urgent lead. Would it be possible to return tomorrow to speak to the rest of the staff?"

He heaved out a sigh. "If you must. I was hoping to get the disruption out of the way today."

"Unforeseen circumstances, sorry. We had every intention wrapping things up here today, but duty calls."

"Don't worry about it. What time will you descend on us again tomorrow?"

"Around eleven, unless anything else turns up in the meantime."

"Is that likely to happen?"

"You never know. Thanks for working with us, Mr Harvey."

"I hope the trip has been worth it?"

"It has. Thanks again."

Katy and Charlie rushed out of the building and back to the car.

"Jesus, that poor man, umm...not Harvey, I meant Salter," Katy said.

Charlie tutted. "Will the CPS be less likely to lay charges at his door in the circumstances?"

Katy nodded. "I should think so. I'll have a word, see if that helps. I think they'll need to put themselves in his shoes. I can't think of anyone who would sit back and not succumb to the threats, do you?"

"True enough. What a terrible predicament to find himself in."

"Yeah, not great. Let's hope it's not too late for his missus."

Charlie held up her crossed fingers. "Amen to that!"

"We'll head back. I think we'll be working overtime tonight, are you up for it?"

"Too bloody right. Will you get an ART involved?"

Katy smiled. "Was that a question or a prod to ensure I go in the right direction, Charlie?"

"Simple question, nothing underhand intended, I swear."

"The first thing I'll do when we get back is run everything past Roberts. He'll have to sanction the overtime anyway."

Charlie nodded. "What's the betting he'll want to be involved in what lies ahead this evening?"

"Yep, I think you're right. I don't mind, as long as he takes a step back and doesn't start issuing orders."

"Is that likely?"

"You don't know Sean Roberts well if you have to ask that, partner."

"Oh heck. In that case, I feel sorry for you having to deal with what's ahead of us."

"If it wasn't for the sanctioning of the overtime, I wouldn't bother paying him a visit."

11

By the time Katy brought DCI Roberts up to date with the information she and Charlie had gathered at the factory, he was chomping at the bit to get involved. "Of course I sanction the overtime, on one proviso," he said.

Katy chuckled. "I warned Charlie you'd want to be involved."

He laughed and pointed at her. "You know me too well, Inspector."

"I do indeed, more's the pity, sir." Katy grinned. "If you'll excuse me, I need to get things organised ASAP."

"Go. Do you need me to throw my weight around?"

"Umm…would you mind organising backup in the form of an ART? We're going to need them."

"Consider it done."

"Thanks. Can you ask the person in charge to contact me personally, if that's not stepping on your toes, sir?"

"I will. Leave it with me. I'll let you know how I get on, soon."

Katy nodded and left the room. She stopped off at the loo and fished out her phone to ring home. "Hi, sorry, I know I should've called you earlier. I'm going to be late."

"I figured something was up. How late? Is everything all right?"

"Yep, Roberts has given overtime the go-ahead for this evening.

The gang are due to make the shipment tonight, so our informant has just told us."

"That's brilliant news. So you're going to catch them in the act, right?"

"We hope so. No telling what time I'll be home, sorry, love."

"Don't be. I'll settle Georgie down with a Disney film, she won't miss you."

"Gee, thanks. Not exactly what a working mother wants to hear."

"You know what I mean. We'll both miss you. Promise me one thing."

"What's that?" She wet her finger and rubbed at the mascara stain under her right eye.

"That you'll stand back and let the team pull their weight for a change."

"I promise. We've got an ART joining us, that should take the pressure off a bit."

"It's put my mind at ease right away. Thank fuck for that. I bet Charlie's excited. This will be her first real test, won't it?"

"She did well today. We had to tackle an absconder, and she was the quickest to react. I have no doubts about her being my partner. I need to push her up the grade ladder ASAP. Not sure having a DC as a partner carries much clout in the eyes of the public."

"I think that's just your perception, love. No one cares what grade a detective is as long as they're good and reliable at their job."

"She's definitely that. Bred from excellent stock, it was to be expected. What dinner am I missing out on tonight?"

"Not sure I should tell you."

"Go on."

"Umm...lasagne."

"Oh crap, my favourite as well. Will it keep?"

"Of course it will. You can either have it when you come home tonight or it'll keep for tomorrow's dinner, no problem."

"Great stuff. I'd hate to think I've missed out on my favourite meal. You're too good to me, AJ."

"I know. It's a good job I love you."

"Right backatcha. I need to go now, need a piddle before I wet myself."

"Thanks for that image of you talking to me while crossing your legs."

"You're welcome. See you later, I hope."

"Stay safe, and don't go getting involved when you don't need to."

"Don't worry about me. It's all in hand, love, I promise. Give Georgie a cuddle from me."

"I will. Love you."

"I love you, too, more than you'll ever realise, AJ."

"I think I know how much. Be safe."

"See you soon, and don't fret about me."

"I'll try not to."

Katy tied up her hair, nipped into a cubicle to empty her bladder, which appeared to be on fire, and then washed her hands. She left the ladies' and bumped into DCI Roberts in the hallway. "Oops...sorry, sir."

"Clumsy of you, Inspector. Why the rush?"

Katy groaned and rolled her eyes. "Because it's all going to kick off in a few hours. I'm just about to call a meeting to discuss what we intend doing about catching these bastards if you fancy attending."

"Music to my ears. Beats going home to a TV dinner and watching those mind-numbing soaps."

"Glad to be of service, sir."

"Come on, let's get on with it."

They entered the bustling incident room, and the noise dimmed instantly.

"Right, team, gather around. I've asked DCI Roberts to join us."

Chairs scraped, and a sense of immense pride suddenly jolted through her. It was replaced quickly by a spike of trepidation which jangled her nerves. She discreetly shook out her arms, hoping to dislodge the tension pulling across her shoulders.

"Everything all right?" Charlie whispered.

"Fine. Weary, that's all. Just trying to get my brain into gear. Okay, listen up, everyone. Charlie and I have just come from the manufacturers of the GPS systems. While we were there we spoke to the owner and the supervisor who assured us that no one on their staff would ever dream of doing anything underhand. Nevertheless, like stubborn bulldogs, Charlie and I forged on regardless. We questioned a gentleman called Aaron Salter who crumbled before our eyes. What he revealed, I have to declare, shocked us. He gave up the name of the man running this gang. The cars are, as we suspected, being stolen with the intent to sell. What we didn't know is the cars are being shipped out to Saudi Arabia tonight at ten o'clock. DCI Roberts has sanctioned overtime for this evening. After the meeting has ended, I need you all to call home, tell your loved ones you'll be late. What have you all managed to find out in our absence?"

Graham was the first to raise his hand. "I've scoured all the footage from the ANPRs in the area surrounding the times the cars were stolen and I believe I've found the lorry they used to transport the vehicles. I can trace its journey so far and then it appears to go off-grid."

"Excellent news, Graham. Any idea what the area consists of where it disappears?"

"It's an industrial estate, boss. I was going to take a ride out there on my way home from work this evening, just to get my facts straight."

"There's no need for that. Google Map the area, that'll give us a rough idea of what to expect. Then I need you and Steve to get over there, we'll put the place under surveillance for the next few hours."

He nodded and gave his partner the thumbs-up.

"Sorry," she said, "I should've said Aaron confirmed the gang leader as Robert Anderton. Now we've had the confirmation, all we know thus far is that he runs an import and export business. The thing is, and this is the most important part in all this, Aaron told us the gang are holding his wife somewhere, forcing his hand to supply the details of where these cars could be picked up from. He's riddled with guilt; however, he's working with us now, so he can't be blamed for what's gone on before. They had him by the short and curlies. So, that's another angle we need to be aware of. Lorraine Salter could be stashed away at a location on our radar this evening, another reason why we should proceed with caution. The chief has arranged for an ART to be on call to help us. I don't think us going in there firing off our Tasers will cut it somehow, do you?"

"Quite right," Roberts chipped in. "I need to make contact with the ART leader later, when we have more facts. He has a team on standby."

"That'd be great. All we have right now is that the cars are scheduled to be at the Port of London at ten this evening. I'm unsure what that time indicates, though. It could mean the cars are going to be delivered at the time or perhaps they're due to set sail then."

"We need to request the port's shipping manifest," Roberts suggested.

"Karen, can you deal with that for me?"

"On it, boss. Do we know the name of the vessel in question?"

Katy shook her head. "Nope. Can you wing it?"

"I'll do my best."

"In the meantime, Charlie and Patrick, I need you guys to find out what you can about Anderton. We need his work and home addresses. I'd like to set up surveillance on him from the word go. I can't imagine him taking a back seat in the proceedings this evening. My guess is he'll want to oversee a job of this magnitude himself." Exhausted, Katy let out a breath.

"Are you okay?" Sean whispered.

She smiled. "I'll let you know how I feel when this is all over. I'm going to arrange a takeaway for everyone. An army can't march on an empty stomach, neither should we."

He dipped his hand in his pocket and pulled out his wallet. "I'll get it. What did you have in mind?"

"Something quick and easy to eat, pizza will do. I need to send some members of the team on their way within an hour or so."

"I agree. Do you want to place the order?"

"I'll get Charlie to do it." She took the fifty Sean was holding out and walked over to Charlie's desk. "Can you order in pizza? Ask everyone what their preference is first."

"Sure. Thanks, boss."

Katy returned to her place beside Sean and whispered, "How did I do?"

He tutted. "I'm going to forget you asked that. Let's get one thing straight, Inspector Foster. If I had one sprinkling of doubt about your work ethics, I wouldn't have appointed you inspector in the first place. So toughen up that skin of yours and get rid of those silly reservations running through your smart brain. Got that?"

Katy's cheeks warmed under his penetrating gaze. "Message received and understood, sir."

*F*orty minutes later, the team were tucking into their pizza at the same time as discussing the final parts of the plan. Charlie and Patrick had come up with addresses for Anderton's home and business. Charlie had also discovered a tenuous link to Thatcham and his partner's business as well. Of course, all that might be circumstantial, but it was definitely something they needed to bear in mind when summing up the case.

"We're stretching the team thin, boss, too many people we need to keep an eye on. We're going to need uniform to lend us a hand on this one."

"I think you're right, however, the last thing we need is a bunch of marked cars showing up."

"Maybe we can use a fleet of unmarked cars for this evening. Do we have that many on site?"

Roberts answered her by dropping his slice of pizza, wiping his hands on a serviette and placing a call to the front desk. "Mick, it's DCI Roberts. How many unmarked cars do we have at our disposal?" He placed the phone on speaker for Katy to hear.

"Off the top of my head, I'd say five at the most, sir."

"Okay, that'll have to do. We're in the process of finalising plans at present, but we're going to need uniform to help us out later, so be prepared. Oh, and we'll need them to use the unmarked vehicles for any surveillance we have in mind."

"I'll put my team on alert. Let me know when and where, and they'll be there, sir."

"Good man. I knew I could count on you."

"Always, sir."

Roberts grinned as he ended the call. "All sorted. We're on a roll, right?"

Katy growled. "Yeah, everything is trundling along nicely. I wouldn't get too cocky about things just yet, if I were you."

"Didn't you know? Cocky is my middle name. Lorne obviously failed to pass on that snippet of information."

Katy stared at him and without thinking said, "Hmm...that particular snippet of information must have slipped her mind. She did tell me a bunch of other stuff, though."

His gaze darted around the room. Katy sensed he was checking to see if the rest of the team had overheard them. They hadn't.

He expelled a breath and leaned in. "That was a mistake."

Katy's eyes widened, and she feigned surprise. "What was?"

His mouth opened and shut, mimicking a fish out of water gasping for the breath that would keep it alive. "It doesn't matter."

She laughed. "Your secret is safe with me, sir."

"Glad to hear it. I was desp—"

Katy raised a hand to cut him off. "I don't want to know the ins and outs of what went on, I haven't got the time, sir."

"That's me told then," he grumbled.

"It's approaching six-thirty. I need to get the surveillance teams organised if we're going to pull this off."

"I agree."

Katy felt relieved he hadn't wanted to pursue the awkward conversation. "Everyone finished their grub?" She glanced around the room at the empty boxes. "Right, let's crack on, time is against us now. Graham and Steve, I need you to head over to try and locate the warehouse. We're still none the wiser about the specific address, so be vigilant when you get close."

The two men nodded and headed towards the door. "We'll keep in touch, boss."

"Do that," she called after them. "Karen, I need you to remain here to man the phones."

"Not a problem, boss."

"That leaves four of us to cover the main targets."

"I'll tag along with you," Roberts was quick to suggest.

Katy stared at Charlie and grimaced. She turned to face Roberts and smiled. "It'll be a pleasure, sir. We'll take Anderton. Charlie and Patrick, I need you to track down Thatcham's partner, Dan Williams' address, just in case he has a part to play in this. Uniform can keep the other members of the gang in their sights. Karen, have you got their names from the research you've gathered?"

"All here, boss."

Roberts took a few paces to his right to collect the information. "Leave this with me, I'll pass the details on to Mick, get him to arrange his team. Do you want them to set off now?"

"Yep, within the next ten minutes, if they can." Katy smiled at Charlie and Patrick. "Any movement from Williams, ring me straight away."

"Want us to get on our way?" Charlie asked, jumping out of her chair.

"Why not? Stay safe, guys. Patrick, keep an eye on her."

Charlie screwed her nose up. "Don't you think that should be the other way around?"

Patrick playfully punched Charlie in the arm. "Cheeky mare. How about we look out for each other?"

Charlie held out her hand for him to shake. "That's a deal."

They left the incident room.

Roberts finished his call and then rubbed his hands together. "That's all organised. I'm quite excited about this. The last time I got involved in a case was when my goddaughter went missing."

"Yep, I remember it well. How is she?"

"Fine and dandy, none the worse for her ordeal. Thanks for asking. I'm eager to get on. Shall we?"

12

"J'm ringing up to see if everything is on course for this evening," Anderton queried.

"It is, boss. All in hand. I told you not to worry."

"I won't stop worrying until those cars are in the middle of the bloody sea. Make sure everything stays on track. Any hint of a derailment and you call me, got that?"

"Of course, boss."

Anderton jabbed a finger at his phone to end the call. He eyed himself in the full-length gold-plated hall mirror and straightened the contrasting white dicky bow to go with his black evening jacket and trousers. Tonight, he hoped, would go down as a special one in his history. He smiled and wiggled his eyebrows. He was ready. The driver was outside, waiting for him. And Paula was expecting him to show up at her door in fifteen minutes.

He left the house, locked it and set the alarm behind him and then entered the limousine.

The driver touched his cap. "Evening, sir."

"Evening, James. Let's get there promptly tonight. I have a table booked at my usual restaurant for seven-forty-five."

"Leave it to me, sir. You just sit back and relax."

James closed the door and got behind the wheel. Celine Dion's dulcet tones escaped the speakers. He knew she was Paula's favourite artist; he was quite partial to the singer himself after seeing her at Caesar's Palace in the States. He rested his head back against the seat, all thoughts of the job about to take place later on that evening pushed to the back of his mind. He'd deal with the intricacies of the job later. Now, though, he needed to concentrate solely on Paula and making her feel special during their dinner.

James pulled up outside the Thatchams' mansion. Anderton's envy gene twitched. *Maybe I could persuade her to…*

Paula was a vision of elegant beauty as she stepped out of the house. Her dress glinted under the lights surrounding the drive to the house.

He hopped out of the car and with the lightest of feet, danced his way towards her. He held out the single red rose, bowed, and then kissed her gently on both cheeks. "You look…well, good enough to eat."

She giggled and slapped his upper arm. "Get away with you. I'm starving. Where are you taking me tonight? And don't disappoint me by saying we're going to the drive-through at Maccies."

"As if I'd dare say that. Don't worry, I have somewhere special lined up for this evening. Come, our table awaits, fair maiden."

"Get out of here," she chided him.

They entered the back of the car as Celine began belting out the theme to *Titanic*. Paula's face lit up. "You remembered."

He slid in beside her, picked up her right hand and kissed the back of it. "Of course I did, was there really any doubt? You've been in my thoughts for days. How are you, my precious lady?"

"Much better now that bastard is no longer in my life. I have a lot to thank you for, Robert."

"Nonsense, I killed him off for both our benefits. He was starting to become a risk to the business. Full of his own self-importance. Thought he could mess me around, he did. Well, I showed him. Now, this time is about us getting to know each other."

"I'm looking forward to that. Of course, I'll still have to make the funeral arrangements and put up a front for that when it finally comes around."

"No news on the pathologist releasing his body yet, then?"

"Not yet. The detective told me they wouldn't do that until they've solved the case."

He raised an eyebrow. "Well, that's not likely to happen anytime soon."

She placed her head against his neck. "Enough talk about him. Let's listen to the music and enjoy our evening. I've been looking forward to this all day."

He squeezed her hand and kissed the top of her head. "So have I." This dinner would be the distraction he needed to keep his mind off the exchange later. He had plans to be there, at the port, ready to take the call for when the transfer of funds hit his account. All trust in his work-force had gone out of the window after what Caves had done. The others knew better than to upset him now, fearing the punishment he might dish out. It was good to keep them on their toes, exhausting but exhilarating at the same time.

He rid his mind of the exchange to concentrate fully on the woman who had stolen his heart the moment he'd laid eyes on her. He'd set out to hook Thatcham back then, to entice him to take a punt working for him on the side as a dealer. He'd tempted him with the girl, ensuring she worked for him and started up the affair that had been both their undoing in the end. Yes, everything had gone according to plan, even down to Thatcham neglecting to fulfil his duties to deliver the heroin at the appointed place the day of his murder.

He had no regrets, no remorse. He was a successful man, used to getting his own way. He wanted this woman, and nothing was about to stand in his way of getting her in his bed.

The restaurant was full, and the intimate atmosphere clearly appealed to Paula. She beamed as soon as she stepped foot inside the luxurious interior. He'd requested a seat in the corner booth. The maître d' seated them and left them to peruse the sumptuous menu for the next five minutes.

"Crikey, it all looks splendid. I'm really not sure what to have. Any suggestions?" Paula asked.

"The turbot is my favourite. Do you want a starter?"

"My waistline says I shouldn't, but what the heck?"

"What about the oysters?"

"Don't they come with a bit of a reputation?"

He wiggled his eyebrows. "They do, which is why I love them."

"And insist on ordering them with your lady friends?" She smirked.

"No, only you. Go on, be brave."

"Okay. If I don't like them then you'll have to eat my share."

"That won't be a problem, I have an insatiable appetite where they're concerned."

He placed the order when the waiter reappeared and then reached for her hand across the table. Her skin was silky smooth and instantly caused a throbbing in his trousers.

"You look beautiful tonight."

"Thank you. Have you had a good day at work?"

"It's been eventful, let's put it that way. It's not over yet. I have to drop by to oversee a delivery at around ten later, if that's all right with you?"

"Oh, does that mean our evening will have to end early?"

"No, not if you don't want it to. You can come with me, and then we could...well, let's not get ahead of ourselves. We'll see how the evening develops and go from there."

Her face lit up.

They chatted about life in general whilst flirting at the appropriate times throughout the meal. For dessert he ordered a special pudding which consisted of a chocolate dome. It was accompanied by a hot fudge sauce.

"Wow, I've never seen anything like this before."

He was chuffed to see the exhilaration lighting up her beautiful features. "It's special. Wait until you see what's inside. Go on...pour the sauce over the top."

She eagerly did as he requested and gasped as the chocolate melted to reveal another glass dome. Inside of that was a velvet box containing a large diamond engagement ring.

"No. This can't be happening." She sat back in her chair, mesmerised by the ring's beauty.

He fiddled with the clasp on the dome, removed the ring and, leaving his chair, dropped to one knee beside her and requested her left hand. He pushed the ring onto her finger and stared into her tear-stained face. "Oh my, tears of joy, I hope."

"They are. You're far too generous. I can't believe how lucky I am to have found you."

Diners on a few of the tables close by applauded. He kissed her and returned to his seat. A swift glance at his watch spoilt the moment for him—it was already nine. Another half an hour and they would need to make a move.

Why is it that the fun times always speed past and yet the bad times tend to linger? I wish I didn't have to go to the damn port tonight.

"Penny for them?" she asked, admiring the ring on her finger.

"Not worth it. Just regretting taking the business decision to be elsewhere later. Speaking of which, another twenty minutes and we're going to have to get on our way."

"That's a shame. Don't feel bad about it, though. These things happen. As someone who used to be dear to me once said, 'business never sleeps'."

He couldn't help wondering if the smart words had come from Ray's mouth. He refused to ask and acquiesced instead. "So true. Drink up, let's enjoy the rest of the bubbly, it would be a shame to waste it."

"Maybe we could take it home with us."

He tipped his head back and roared. "I'm sure they'd love that."

A little while later, he grudgingly searched his watch for the time and tutted. "Time to go. I'll settle the bill."

He left the table and returned once he'd paid for the meal and added a hefty tip into the bargain. He held out an arm, and she slipped hers through it once she stood.

"I've had a wonderful evening, just what I needed." She beamed, and he kissed the tip of her nose.

"It's not over yet, darling." Her smile captivated his hard heart, instantly melting it.

He'd never anticipated ever feeling such raw emotions about a woman, but here he was, a quivering wreck in her presence.

Anderton escorted her outside. The chauffeur had the back door open, awaiting their arrival. Anderton eased her into the seat, gave the driver brief instructions of where to go next and slid in beside her.

She placed a hand on his thigh, and a shiver of excitement rippled through him. One final hurdle to leap through for the day, and then he'd whisk the lady back home and…

∼

*K*aty and Sean had followed Anderton to the restaurant. Katy was left shaking her head when she saw Paula Thatcham get in the car with the businessman.

During their two-hour stake out of the restaurant, Katy had been organising her team from the car, receiving regular updates from Graham about the comings and goings at the warehouse. Charlie had reported that things were all quiet as far as Dan Williams was concerned, leading Katy to believe she may have done the man an injustice, thinking he was involved in the setup.

In between calls, Roberts was in regular contact with the commanding officer of the ART. Everything was in place and ready to rock and roll. Butterflies had taken flight in Katy's stomach and were dive-bombing each other judging by the sensation she was feeling.

Anderton and Thatcham left the restaurant and entered the back of his limo.

"They seem all loved up," she stated, bitterness entering her tone.

"Hard to think she's a grieving widow, right?"

"Yeah, that part has never washed with me. She was too quick to accuse the other woman when I spoke to her about her husband's death. Shame on her if she was in on it."

"It definitely seems that way to me. She'll get what's coming to her, they all will. They can't cause the disruption they have in this city and not expect to suffer the consequences."

She nodded and slotted the car into gear as the limo set off. "Let's hope we can pull this off tonight and nothing major goes wrong."

"Have faith. If we were dealing with the bastards ourselves then I would have my doubts, knowing the weapons they have at their disposal. But having the backup we have in place should put our minds at ease when the time arises to swoop on the bastards."

"I hope you're right. I hate not being in control."

"I don't get it, you are in control. I haven't taken over at all."

She shrugged. "I wasn't getting at you. I was referring to the response team. They'll strip me of control once they get involved."

"You just have to accept that, Katy. We're not armed. These guys are the most dangerous we've come across in years, it's the only way to deal with them, believe me."

"I know, it's me being silly, ignore me."

They followed the limo through the lit streets of the capital out to the port.

"Are you ready for it all to kick off?" she asked Roberts.

"We'll see. Hold back, we don't want to alert them, and the traffic is thinning now we're this far out."

"Thanks for the advice. Maybe you hadn't noticed the engine die down a little about two miles back."

"Sarcastic bitch. I heard, I was merely pointing out the obvious."

"You don't say." She faced him and grinned.

The limo slowed down and stopped in front of her.

She switched off her lights, pulled over and surveyed her surroundings. "I'm not liking this. Do you think they spotted us?"

"Who knows? Right, don't panic. Let's get things in place. You call Charlie and Graham, see if there's any movement there, and I'll get in touch with the commander."

Katy made the calls, her gaze glued to the limo. The way it was sitting there made her jittery. Graham told her that there was no other news to add except that the Range Rover had left thirty minutes before. He'd already informed her of that detail, however.

Charlie sounded bored when she rang her. "Nothing. All the lights are on in his flat, he's not stepped foot outside since he arrived home."

"Okay, thanks. We're at the port now, waiting on the ART to join us. The boss is organising that now. Hold fire and stay alert. I've got a strange feeling about this that I just can't put my finger on."

"I hear you," Charlie replied. "Stay safe."

"You, too. Don't worry about us. I'm in safe hands with the boss nearby." She ended the call and grinned at Sean.

He sniggered. "You reckon."

Just then the door flew open, and Sean was dragged from the car. Katy scrabbled for her phone but dropped it in her haste before she, too, was wrenched out of the driver's seat. They were both marched by two of Anderton's henchmen towards the limo. Katy glanced over her shoulder and spotted the Range Rover sitting behind her car off to the left. She'd taken her eye off the ball, distracted by the phone calls she'd made. Checking in with the damn team had allowed the bastards to sneak up on her.

Roberts grunted ahead of her as the bloke manhandling him punched him in the gut and leaned in to issue a threat.

"Leave him alone, you bastard," she shouted, engaging her mouth before her damn brain.

The goon holding her arm jabbed her in the solar plexus. She doubled over and groaned.

"Now are you gonna keep your mouth shut?" her assailant demanded.

She stood upright, summoning up her courage and strength and narrowed her eyes at the thug. "Screw you."

He swiped her face, sending her head ricocheting first off to the left and then the right. "Mouth shut, bitch, or you'll get more of the same. We don't hold back just 'cos you're a cop. If anything, we'll treat you worse, so my advice would be to button it."

Shit! I'd better do as he says. Fuck, where are the team? They should be here by now.

Her gaze darted around the area, discreetly searching for any sign. Over to the right she sensed movement, but nothing came of it. They were within spitting distance of the limo now. The driver left his seat and opened the back door. A smug-looking Anderton emerged and glared at them.

"Well, well, well, what do we have here? Two nosy officers of the law. What do you know, guys? Maybe we can have some fun with them before…"

Thankfully, Roberts remained quiet, as did Katy. Her thoughts were with her team, willing them to come to their rescue. A sinking feeling in the pit of her stomach told her the odds were against her, and she couldn't help wondering what Anderton had meant by 'before'. Was his intention to kill them?

Oh God, don't let him give the all clear for his goons to rape me, not in front of Sean!

Anderton came to within a few inches of her and Sean. "Nothing to say for yourselves?" he sneered. "You think you can follow me and expect me not to notice? What type of cops are you? Keystone comes to mind." He laughed at his own joke.

Paula Thatcham emerged from the back of the limo.

Anderton held out his hand for hers. "Come join me, my love. Now, what do you think we should do with our guests?"

Paula's gaze avoided Katy's, and she shrugged. "No idea. I want nothing to do with this."

"It's too late, Paula, we know you're involved. You disposed of your husband, that's what started this investigation off. It was only a matter of time before we discovered the intricacies of your combined plan," Katy shouted.

Paula's mouth opened and shut.

Anderton flung an arm around her shoulder. "Ha, call yourself a detective? She had nothing to do with this. I killed off her old man. He deserved to die after cheating on her. You think she warranted scum like that doing the dirty on her? No. I made it my mission to dispose of him. All right, my men screwed up, it was my intention to steal his boat, but don't worry, my men were punished for fucking up."

"I didn't want him killed off. I would have left him, eventually," Paula said, a deep frown wrinkling her pale brow.

He took her hands in his and smiled. "He wronged me, more importantly, he wronged you, my love. You deserve to be treated like a princess, he neglected to do that."

"Most of the time he was good to me."

"Most of the time...our future will centre around me *always* treating you right."

"If you're prepared to do anything for me then let the officers go."

He stared at her, shock set into the wrinkles around his eyes. "What? Why? I need this transaction to go ahead this evening. It'll be the making of us. If I let them go, they'll jeopardise everything."

Paula shook her head. "I don't want any part of this. I haven't got a clue what your intentions are but I want nothing to do with it." She walked back towards the car. "Driver, take me home."

Katy saw something glint off to the right. Her gaze homed in and spotted an armed officer taking aim. She glanced at Sean. He was watching her. She mouthed discreetly, "Follow my lead."

She bowed her head low and wrenched her arm out of the goon's hand and ran at the other bloke holding Sean. He did the same and head-butted the thug who'd been guarding Katy. Shots were fired.

Anderton's men withdrew their guns and returned fire on the ART. In the melee, Katy shouted for Sean to run with her. They managed to make it behind one of the containers before bullets came hurtling towards them as Anderton ordered his men to attack.

"Are you okay?" she asked.

"I think I got hit." He stared down at his hand covered in blood.

"Shit! Where?" Katy forgot all about the danger surrounding them and tended to the gaping wound in his side. She tore off her jacket and pressed it on to the wound. "This is going to hurt. I want you to know I take little pleasure in doing this, sir."

Sean's smile was faint, and he whispered, "I believe you, Inspector. Save yourself, Katy. Don't worry about me."

"No way. We're in this together." She peered around the edge of the container. Shots lit up the darkness, and the noise almost deafened her. Then there was silence.

Why? What the hell was going on? She peeked around the corner again. Anderton and his goons were sprawled out on the concrete. The driver was kneeling beside the vehicle, his hands behind his head amidst shouted commands from the ART.

A car screeched to a halt behind Katy's. It was Charlie.

Katy's voice sounded strained as she called out to her partner. "Over here, Charlie. Get an ambulance. We need help."

Charlie hurtled towards her, speaking into her phone as she ran, Patrick not far behind her. "My God, what happened?"

Relief swept through Katy. "It's Sean, he's been hit, he's losing a lot of blood."

"Fuck!" Charlie shouted. "The ambulance is on its way. We heard over the radio that shots had been fired and left our post, I'm sorry."

"Nonsense. You did the right thing." Katy swept a stray strand of hair off Sean's forehead. "Are you all right, Sean?"

"I think so. How long?"

"Not long. I can hear them approaching now. Stay with us, don't you fall asleep now." It was too late, his eyes slipped shut. "Sean, Sean, don't you dare die."

"Leave him to me." Charlie swivelled Sean off Katy's lap and, laying him flat on the ground, she began CPR. "Don't you dare give up on us, Sean Roberts. What the fuck would Lorne say if you gave up now?"

Pump, pump, pump.

The sirens wailed and got ever nearer.

Katy leapt to her feet. "Patrick, direct them to us. Hurry."

He bolted out to the road, and within seconds, two paramedics appeared carrying bags.

"All right, what have we got?" the older male paramedic asked.

"Gunshot wound to the side. Charlie has been giving him CPR. Please, you have to save him. Don't let him die."

"I'll do my best. Tracy, keep up the CPR."

The female paramedic took over from Charlie who stood and clutched Katy's hand. "I did my best."

"You did. I'm sure he'll be fine." Katy watched the male paramedic inject a clear liquid into Sean's vein. Her heart was heavy now. On the verge of tears, she watched the paramedics work hard and fast to revive him.

The defibrillator was unveiled from one of the bags. The female ripped open Sean's shirt and attached the paddles. His whole body jolted as the surge ran through him, not once but twice.

Charlie glanced at Katy. Katy shook her head, fearing the worst. She offered up a silent prayer to her maker.

Please, God, don't let this good man die, not here, not now, not like this!

Her prayers were answered when the male paramedic shouted, "I've got a pulse. All right, let's get him stabilised and back to the hospital. Does anyone want to come along for the ride?"

"Yes, me," Katy shouted in her excitement at seeing Sean's chest rise and fall as it should do. "Charlie, the keys are in the car. So is my mobile, will you get that for me?"

Charlie sprinted to the vehicle and returned. She held out Katy's phone and smiled. "I'm glad he's all right. Don't worry about your car, it's all in hand."

"Don't let the driver get away. Also, Paula Thatcham is in the back of the limo. Take her in for questioning. I'm not sure if she had anything to do with this or whether she was spouting her innocence just for our benefit. We'll interview her all the same. I'll ring you with an update when I can."

"Want me to ring AJ?"

Katy held up her phone. "No, I'll do it."

EPILOGUE

"*H*e'll be surprised to see us," Katy said, marching along the corridor with a bunch of hospital-bought flowers in her hand.

"Depends if that's a good or bad surprise," Charlie replied. She pushed open the door to the men's ward.

"We'll soon find out." Katy winked at her.

They walked the length of the ward and stopped at the bottom of the bed closest to the window. Sean Roberts opened his eyes, sensing their presence.

"Ah, my two favourite officers. Come to visit your injured superior, have you?"

Katy stepped forward and placed the flowers on the bedside cabinet. She hesitated, wondering whether she should kiss him on the cheek or not.

He must have been aware of what was running through her mind because he raised his cheek and pointed at it. "You may kiss me. Only if you want to, though."

"Will it go in my favour with any further promotions?"

"Cheeky mare." Roberts laughed then winced and placed a hand over his injured side.

"Sorry, didn't mean to make you laugh. How are you?"

"Doc says I should be out of here in a few days. I don't have to tell you how bored rigid I am being in this damn bed."

"Nope. It's a necessity. A few days? You won't be back at work anytime soon, will you?"

He cocked an eyebrow. "Wanna bet? I've already spoken to the super. He's given me the all clear to return to the station."

"Bloody hell, Sean...sorry, sir, give yourself a break."

"I'm fine. Eager to get back behind my desk. Don't worry about me. Tell me what's been happening regarding the investigation."

Katy and Charlie sat on either side of the bed.

Sean's focus remained on Katy.

"Well," Katy said, "after we questioned Paula, she broke down in tears and admitted she knew that Anderton had killed her husband but is swearing blind she had nothing to do with his murder."

"Do you believe her?" Roberts asked through narrowed eyes.

"The jury is still out for me, especially after she admitted Anderton had just slipped an engagement ring on her finger. Distasteful bugger it is, too."

"What? She got engaged to Anderton? Her bloody husband only died a few days ago, for fuck's sake."

"Exactly. However, we've got nothing to tie her to the murder, not yet, although I intend to keep digging. I'll run it past the CPS, see if they can offer any guidance on the matter."

"The nerve of the frigging bitch. She must have had something to do with his murder. What decent woman would accept another man's ring before her former husband was buried?"

"Hard to figure out. Maybe she felt what the heck after finding out Ray had cheated on her."

He shook his head and tutted. "Bloody women—sorry, present company excepted, of course. Oh, ignore me, I'm just being a grumpy old divorced geezer."

"You said it," Katy replied. "Anyway, she swears blind she had no knowledge of the transaction that was about to go down. Again, something in the way she portrayed herself during the interview caused me to doubt she was telling the truth. Without solid proof or any evidence to the contrary, there's not a lot we can do about it."

"Don't give up on her, go with your gut if you need to. Put twenty-four-hour surveillance on her if necessary."

"What would be the point? Oh God, you don't know, do you?"

"Know what?"

She grinned and then twisted her mouth before she spoke. "The ART did a number on Anderton and his gang. They were all killed at the port."

Sean clenched his fist and punched the bed beside him. "Great, not the news I was expecting to hear. I was hoping we'd get our day in court with those bastards. What about the cars?"

"All safe and returned to the families."

"That's one thing at least."

"Oh, and we found Lorraine Salter tied to a chair at the warehouse. She had a bomb strapped to her chest. The disposal team deactivated it and set her free, and she was reunited with her husband, Aaron, who has supplied us with a full confession. I think that covers everything, the only thing left to fathom out is how the gun was lifted from our evidence room and found its way into the hands of these criminals. Okay, enough about work, is there anything we can get for you?"

"I don't suppose you have half a bottle of whisky or brandy in that handbag of yours, do you?"

"Nope, and even if I had, I wouldn't hand it over."

"Spoilsport. I need something to brighten my day. I thought about flirting with the nurses but discovered my heart wasn't in it. Maybe it's going to take me more time than I anticipated to get over Carmen."

"Talking of which, I was wondering if I should ring her, let her know you're in hospital. What do you think?"

"Don't you dare. The last thing I need or want is her sympathy."

"I wasn't really thinking about her, I was thinking of Sara. She'd want to visit her daddy, surely."

"Maybe. No, leave well alone. I'm supposed to be seeing her on Sunday, I'll tell her then."

"If you're sure. Okay, I hate to run out on you like this, but we should be making a move. Lots of paperwork to catch up on, and our ogre of a boss is a bit tied up at the moment…"

"Go, get out of here. Thanks for visiting and bringing me up to date on things. Oh, and, Charlie, I bet your mum is going to have a good laugh about this when you tell her."

"Umm…she already knows and er…sends you her love and told me to pass on her best wishes, sir."

A smile stretched his dry lips apart. "Thanks, that's cheered me up."

Katy and Charlie left the hospital and returned to the station to let the team know that Sean was bearing up and would be back on duty soon.

*T*he day which Katy had been dreading all week dawned. She dressed Georgie in a pretty pink summer dress and then went through dozens of outfits in her wardrobe until she finally settled on a cream dress and jacket she had worn to one of her friends' wedding a few years before. "How do I look?" She asked AJ, twirling in the kitchen.

"Beautiful as ever, except for the slippers, you might want to ditch them."

Katy poked her tongue out at him.

Georgie came bounding into the kitchen carrying her favourite doll. "Mummy, you look bootiful."

Katy leaned down and kissed her daughter on the cheek. "That makes two of us."

"I'm a lucky man." AJ beamed.

Katy scrutinised his attire up and down. "You're not wearing that, are you?"

"What's wrong with it? Jeans and a casual shirt. Oh no, don't tell me I have to dress up? It's nearly ninety degrees out there."

"Yeah, and your point is?"

He shook his head and stomped out of the room. He reappeared wearing his cream linen suit a few minutes later. "Will I do now?"

"Daddy, now you look bootiful, too."

He picked Georgie up and spun his giggling daughter around on the spot. Katy smiled. This was a moment to cherish. She just hoped they were still in good spirits by the end of the day.

"Come on, let's get this over with. I mean, let's visit Nanny and Granddad."

AJ placed his daughter on the floor and wrapped an arm around each of them. "Whatever happens today, I have all the family I want around me."

*A*J drove, and they arrived at the country estate his parents owned a little after twelve. The traffic had held them up. Hardly the best start to what Katy thought would be a fraught day.

AJ's mother stood on the steps, awaiting their arrival.

"We'll let Georgie go first, she'll help break the ice." AJ patted Katy on the knee.

"Good idea. Come on, let's face the music."

AJ got out of the car and released Georgie from her car seat. "Go see Nanny, sweetheart."

"Nanny, Nanny, Nanny." Georgie ran up the steps and flung herself into her grandmother's arms.

"Georgie, my precious child. My, don't you look pretty?"

Katy and AJ held hands and climbed the steps to join them just in time to hear Georgie say, "It's the dress I wanted to wear to Mummy and Daddy's wedding, but Mummy said I couldn't."

"Oh, have you two set the date then?" AJ's mother asked, misunderstanding what Georgie had said.

AJ held up his hand to show off his wedding band. "No, we got married last week, Mother."

Cecilia's face darkened with anger until Georgie asked, "What's wrong, Nanny? You don't look well."

"Not in front of Georgie, Mother. It wouldn't be fair," AJ warned.

"You'd better come in. Let's see what your father has to say about this." She turned, still carrying Georgie, and stepped through the large double front doors.

AJ glanced at Katy.

She touched his face with her hand. "Stay strong."

"Reginald, where are you? Our visitors have arrived," his mother shouted, unladylike.

"I'll be out in a moment. Go into the garden, I'll be with you as soon as I've finished my phone call."

Once they were in the garden, Cecilia asked them abruptly, "Drink?"

"Thanks, we'll have a non-alcoholic one, if you don't mind," Katy said.

Cecilia glared at her and went back into the house.

"I'm not liking this one bit," Katy said.

"We knew it wasn't going to be easy, love."

"Don't take any shit, AJ. Any sign of trouble and we're out of here. Life's too short for this sort of crap."

"Okay, don't be negative, let's see how things progress for now."

"What the…?" AJ's father bellowed in the hallway.

AJ bent down and whispered in Georgie's ear. "Go see Granddad, sweetie."

Georgie ran through the patio doors calling for her granddad.

"Shame on you for using your daughter like that." Katy sniggered.

"I'm willing to try every trick going if it'll help. Remind me whose idea it was to come here today?"

"Yours."

"Why do you always listen to me?"

"Because you're wise," Katy replied.

"Not this time."

AJ's mother and father appeared with Georgie running ahead of them.

"Hello, Father."

"Son, Katy. Nice to see you both. I hear congratulations are in order."

AJ nodded. "Yes, I suppose they are, sir."

AJ's father held out his arms for Katy to walk into. "Congratulations, I wish you'd given us the chance to attend," he whispered in her ear.

Katy gulped down the saliva filling her mouth. "It was a spur-of-the-moment thing. We're sorry, sir."

"What's done is done. Where's the champagne, Cecilia?"

"But they wanted non-alcoholic drinks."

"Nonsense. It's time for us to celebrate. You'll all have to stay the night if you get too drunk, won't you?" Reginald let out a roaring laugh.

Katy offered to help AJ's mother, but she refused and scurried back into the house.

"She'll come around. It's about time you two did the deed. I'm delighted for you both."

"Thanks, Dad, that means a lot."

"Now, I won't say I'm not disappointed, but we'll get past it. Give your mother time to get used to the idea."

"Thank you, sir," Katy said, feeling a little more relaxed.

Georgie ran off into the garden, chasing a couple of butterflies as Cecilia rejoined them and handed over the bottle of champers to AJ's father to open.

"Now the little one is out of earshot, I need to say my piece. Quite frankly, I'm devastated by the news. Did your parents attend the wedding?" she demanded, turning to face Katy.

"No, in fact, we haven't even told them yet. We thought we'd share the news with you first."

"Well, I suppose that's something." Cecilia took a step towards her son and held out her arms. "Why do you do this to us, AJ?"

He stepped into his mother's embrace. "I'm a grown man, Mother, I make my own decisions in life now."

Cecilia hugged him and then did the same to Katy. "Welcome to the family, Katy. Make him happy, won't you?"

"We've been together over five years, Cecilia, never a cross word between us."

"Good, keep it that way."

Reginald passed the champagne around. "To the happy couple. May they present us with more adorable grandchildren in the near future."

Katy and AJ looked at each other and smiled.

Now that's a conversation to be held another day. Not right now, though!

THE END

Note to you the reader.

Thank you for reading the first book in the Justice Again series, I'm hoping you'll agree with me that Katy and Charlie make a phenomenal team.

Next up for the team is a heart-wrenching tale which I guarantee will tug on your heart strings.

Pick up your copy of ULTIMATE DILEMMA here.

As always, thank you so much for your continued support of my work, none of this would be possible without my readers and fans behind me. If you could spare five minutes to leave a review if you enjoyed Gone in Seconds, I'll forever be in your debt.

Until our paths meet again, stay safe and happy reading.
M A Comley.

KEPT IN TOUCH WITH M A COMLEY

Newsletter
http://smarturl.it/8jtcvv

BookBub
www.bookbub.com/authors/m-a-comley

Blog
http://melcomley.blogspot.com

Join my special Facebook group to take part in monthly giveaways.

Readers' Group

Printed in Poland
by Amazon Fulfillment
Poland Sp. z o.o., Wrocław